I ONCE WAS

J C PEREIRA

DEDICATION

I dedicate this book to those who haven't yet closed their eyes.

CONTENTS

ACKNOWLEDGMENTS

Many authors have previously explored this theme. As a young man, I read a book portraying one of the old gods down on his luck and eking out an existence on the streets of our cities. My thanks to this writer for his influence. I also owe a great deal to an informative, moving documentary called 'Gypsy Child Thieves'. I recommend it to anyone who needs to be enlightened on this subject.

PROLOGUE

The wooden door crashed inwards. An act of explosive and intrusive violence. The sharp sound of splintered wood cracking around the room. The two women within froze, stunned into petrified silence and immobility. Their domestic harmony and private space shattered and violated. The two small children, still at their sleepy breakfast, now thoroughly aroused in terror, stared wide-eyed with incomprehension at the rude and uninvited invaders. The threat they all felt was a stark and solid emotional slap in the face. It awakened them, overcame them, suspending their reality. All that was left behind to show a morning just like any other were the scattered bread crumbs on the table and floor.

'Move, all of you! Get out! Get out!'

The rough, unshaven men that smelt so strongly of stale sweat and aggression were pitiless. Gesticulating with their oiled guns, they pointed to the broken door, shoving and pushing roughly the bewildered occupants out of their shelter, their home, exposing them to the uncaring street beyond. The children, a beautiful girl of seven and her little sister of two years, clutched their mother and aunt's hands in desperate grips. They sensed that what was happening was outside of the control of their guardians but still, in their innocence, trusted in the protection of their elders. The women, wise to the vagaries of fate, knew they had no helping hand to count on and sought safety in submissiveness. They tried to behave normal in a situation that was far from that.

 With the little girls tagging along obediently, they were pushed to their knees in the dirt, with their foreheads pressed against the brick wall of a corner house. Here they were blindfolded, even the children, by the brutal deftness of men who had long ago lost their souls and felt that they had nothing else to lose. The women, nurturers, comforters, carers, the heart of hearth and home, knew what was coming. They reached out with blind, open palms to clasp and anchor the lost and spinning emotions of their small, cherished loved ones, gathering them to the warmth of their bodies one last time. As the sharp cracks of gunfire echoed twenty-two times into the frightened morning, four lives were snuffed out of existence, without even being offered the courtesy as to the reason why. An incident, sudden, brutal and final.

 He watched it all. The heavy thumping in his chest telling him that he was still alive. He felt their loneliness in the face of this gross atrocity. He felt the confused and panicked emotions of the little ones, contained only within their tiny rib-cages by the steadiness and acceptance of their mother and aunt. He could almost hear the words that might have been whispered, 'Don't worry. It will be alright.' We lie to our children to hide our own fears. He was a father, wasn't he? He knew the truth of it more than most. They had not called to him. Why? Simple. Should they have done so? Had they forgotten him? No, more than that. They did not know him.

 He watched it all and felt the hot tear force its way through the crack in the seal around his eye.

CHAPTER I

The foul smell of his breath mixed with alcohol, the stench of his unwashed clothes and the growing rumble of fast moving traffic brought him floundering from the depths of drowning in spiralling dreams. The harsh, rushing glare of headlights made him squeeze his eye shut in an attempt to save his brain from being pierced by the stabbing shards of light. What was that last dream? It was already gone. He couldn't bring it back. He couldn't even recall his own name. Had he ever had one? With a large dirty hand which he had the fleeting impression was once filled with strength, he wiped his bearded face and felt the wetness of tears in the matted hair. He fought down the rising feeling of disgust and staggered to his feet, stepping back quickly onto the long curb that formed an island as a machine of destruction, horn blaring in a fury, nearly ran him over.

'Bastaror!' he muttered under his breath.

The one following fast in its wake doused him with brown, cold water, soaking his already damp trousers right through to his skin. He hardly seemed to notice and bent over to retrieve his bundle of sodden blankets. Then, as if he had forgotten what he was about to do, he straightened his spine and walked off, leaving his pitiful belongings behind, stumbling between the pillars that separated both sides of the dual underpass, the sound of the racing vehicles on either side striving to crush his eardrums. He paid them no heed but wandered along in a world of his own. Grainy moisture coated every surface and dripped from the ceiling way up in the darkness above. A sure recipe for bronchial illnesses of every description and eventually pneumonia but not for this man who had spent years wandering around this city of God. Through the baking heat of its summers, through its cold, damp winters, its unforgiving torrential downpours and its stunning spring days and carefree nights. The majority of the time he moved or sat in areas where he stayed unnoticed, especially by those whose sole purpose was to enjoy the delights of the Eternal City. On those odd chances when he was noticed, he dimly registered the guarded looks of pity, revulsion and even anger. These paltry things did not touch him, and on the rare occasions that they did, they were promptly forgotten. His senses were dulled to the point of unfeeling.

Emerging from the tunnel, he appeared to make a random turn, drifting unhurriedly across the path of the oncoming traffic, showing an unconcerned face to the swerving, squealing cars and the outraged honking of strident horns.

'Cazzo!' was the chorus of calls that followed his suicidal, plodding progress.

It wasn't worth the time of the good citizens to run down a homeless 'barbone' but even so, his presence on their streets was a frightening reminder of the vulnerabilities of life. They preferred that he remained unseen in the shadows rather than parade his sordid message of failure.

The city was still imbued with near-sighted greyness as the shaggy creature, floppy felt hat rammed low around his hairy ears, picked his way unerringly through the back streets running alongside the ghostly train station, floating forlornly in the early morning winter's fog. He instinctively avoided the regular patrols now that this once haven had become off-limits to those such as he, not because he was afraid of them but because he wanted to avoid all challenges. It stirred something nasty deep inside him, and he didn't want whatever it was to come out. It was then that he saw them. Lurking at the next corner with that sickening halo glowing around their sanctimonious heads. He was not hungry and anyway he found it impossible to swallow the essence of the god that seeped out of them. It made his stomach heave. He turned and crossed the street to avoid them. Their eyes caught him and followed him silently, a look of patience and benediction in their gaze. They did not call to him. They had given that up many years ago. Their paths would cross again in this small city. He hated it here. It made him feel weaker than in any other place, but here he could hide. Here he could hide from the potency of those dreams which of course, he could never remember but which haunted him afterwards, nevertheless. He wanted to die and sometimes found himself wondering for days what death really was. Some fast talking fool, skinnier than a shade, tried to convince him one night in the sheltered arch of an ancient building during a severe thunderstorm that somehow brought him comfort, that he had the answer to blissful death whilst still living. In an attempt to get rid of the nuisance or at least shut him up, he allowed the talkative idiot to stick a needle in his arm and inject a black, tar-like, liquid substance that smelled of vinegar. It helped him to lose a day or two but made his unwelcomed dreams even more vivid. Talk, as he always knew, was cheap and in many cases, useless. Try as he did, he still could not remember what happened to the fool, and he could not recall ever meeting him again.

With the servants of the God successfully evaded, he embarked on a long and circuitous route leading to the river. By now the roads were becoming crowded as people spilt out of the shiny holes that served as entrances to the tunnels they had dug beneath their city, many stopping to gulp down a thick, hot stimulant to help them face the unnatural world they had created around them and now could not avoid. As he passed these places, he would on a whim, whip off his hat and hold it out. Most times he was ignored, but now and again, someone would drop a coin in, hastily slinking off with a distracted air, unwilling to show any sign of engagement. He never stopped, always keeping on the move, for these places were jealously guarded by organised beggars who mysteriously materialised at every bar, cafeteria or bakery that did good business. This city was like an onion, it had many layers, but then so did all the other cities. A myriad of images flashed through his mind then disappeared before he could hold onto them. He knew that he had been to many places, but that was all that he knew. The lack of memory was both a curse and a blessing.

A little girl filled with the wisdom of innocence looked directly into his eye with her clear brown ones and smiled, holding up a tiny hand to him. Immediately, her mother pulled her away out of reach and the word 'schifo' drifted in on the breeze. Oh, the price of wisdom. A gust of wind stirred the discarded pieces of paper littering the broad pavement and a torn, dirty page from a travel brochure highlighting the beauty of the northern fjords with a stunning photograph on display, distracted his attention. He bent, picked it up and stuffed it in his pocket. 'Ye shall seek me, and shall not find me; where I am, thither ye cannot come.' Where did that come from? It smelt of the God. He had spent his whole life seeking for something but what? The answer lay somewhere in the dark pit that was his mind.

On cue, the grey/brown clouds above rolled in out of nowhere. They opened their heavy robes and dumped a deluge down on the city, attempting to wash the dirt and the smell of the dog piss away. Splashing through the racing rivulets that soaked his feet, he observed the miraculous thing of selfie stick sellers instantly transforming into brolly vendors. Magic always made him want to smile, but he couldn't remember the last day that he had done so.

It was in this moment of transitional chaos when everyone dived to shelter themselves and theirs, that he glimpsed the boy across the street make his move. Quick as a wink, he snatched two peaches from the open-fronted fruit shop and in one smooth motion, stuffed them under his coat and continued on his way. He saw the past, the present, and the future in that one action and remembered something long forgotten. The pain was unbearable as it split open the side of his skull; the taste of the cold, clean rain-water, bitter on his lips.

CHAPTER II

He was an asset. He knew it. They all knew it. He had learnt the ropes from his sister since he was nine. She had been the best of the best. A master of the cash-points. She was so valuable that her bride price at thirteen had been seven-thousand euros. True, part of it was because she was an untouched virgin, a great cause for celebration, but the greater part was due to her profitability. His uncle and aunt had been over the moon at the time but now turned their eyes on him to take over the top job. He had immediately given up begging and started targeting the bancomats; fifty euros per day against six-hundred, sometimes a thousand, was no contest at all. Then things started to go wrong with the burgeoning family enterprise. His sister was gone. Three nights after her wedding and the public airing of her blood, the police had come. They had been watching them, clocking their movements and activities like the bloody snoops that they were. His uncle and aunt were shut away in the clink, and he had been handed over to the two-faced child-protection agency. It didn't take him long to give the careless bastards the slip, but when he eventually made his way back to the camp, it was gone. Bulldozed into piles of rubble. All that was left were the rats.

Now he was with rats of a bigger and nastier variety, but he was doing much better out of it than he had before. Wandering around after finding his home and family gone, he had felt lost. He was the first to admit that. His sister and her new family had disappeared, scarpered like mice into the city fabric and he had had nowhere to go. Within an hour, however, a car piloted by his kind, that is, people from his home country but not of his kin, had picked him up in their Mercedes-Benzes SUV. Better the devil you know, as the saying goes. He was driven to an innocuous apartment block on the outskirts of the city, just a short bus ride from where he had once spent his short life. A place he had not known even existed. Here he was introduced to an army of other children from a mixture of clans, all bereft of earlier ties, their strings cut by the misunderstanding actions of a prejudiced state. That was the way of it. No point in crying like a baby. They were all around his age, now twelve, almost a man, both boys and girls. Caring for them with possessive eyes were about eight minders, young men and women between twenty and thirty years but it was hard to tell for certain as us folks live hard and short lives that lay a heavy hand on our features. We were all grouped into working pairs or threes with a designated point to report to and drop off our earnings. It was well organized, and we each were familiar with our duty. We knew what was expected or else. Better that than being imprisoned in a bloody school and being bullied and called names all day long. He now belonged to a new family of about fifty. The unwanted, the dregs of the dregs but we will all get rich and build big villas back home. That was the plan.

It didn't take long for his controllers to get the message that he worked better alone. He was strong for his age, aggressive and determined but most of all he was clever and could wear whatever skin the situation demanded at the drop of a hat. He was 'spesh'; a bloody chameleon. He was also without fear and this in a way, made them wary of him. Unfortunately, this had its downside for they were specifically more brutal in their reprimands and when they suspected he was holding out on them. He would state his innocence without any sign of emotion, no matter how hard they beat him and most disconcerting of all, he would look them calmly in the eye whilst doing so. Since, of course, he did hold out on them more often than not, he was growing rich on the sly. Still, they allowed him to keep a larger share of his earnings than the others despite their suspicions, for they did not want to push him into scarpering off to another clan. This was, naturally, against the law of the people but he was valuable, and profit was everything. They worked him like a dog, ten hours a day, but he had them where he wanted them for as they kept saying, 'You're a clever bastard.' Yes, he was, and his secretly hidden stashes were growing alongside his ego and confidence.

He had caught an early tube ride and was on his way to his favourite hunting fields. The early bird and all that. The station guard behind his protective glass knew him well and couldn't even be bothered to stir a finger and shout at him when he jumped over the ticket barrier. The fat, old fool had already surrendered to the futility of running after him.

'Gypsy piece of shit,' he could hear him mutter, and laughed, waving insolently at the corpulent idiot.

The buggers outside were so preoccupied in contemplating the upcoming stress in their day that they were already distracted and he anticipated lifting a few careless wallets and purses before he got to his destination. No sleight of hand needed here. Just choose an opportune mark and help yourself. Take, take, take. Just like in a candy shop. His controller was still snoring his head off on his mattress and would rise in a foul mood when he discovered that he had already gone. He would get a few blows to the head for his independent thinking, but there was a price for everything in this life. These extras acquired would be his and his only; a sweet and delightful balm to overcome the bruising discomfort of a knock or two. Nevertheless, he was happy, and he had a bounce in his stride when the shitty heavens opened up and bucketed down on him. 'With every disappointment, there is a blessing,' his sister used to say, so with the God sent distraction he helped himself to some breakfast fruit. The silly shop owner, caught with his pants down, was so busy pulling across his awning that he didn't have a clue that his tray was a little lighter. Then, suddenly, he felt a chill run up and down his spine and hurriedly glanced around him like a cock which had just heard the fox outside his hen-house. Through the sheeting torrential rainfall, he glimpsed the figure of a tall, grey-haired barbone. With such poor visibility, it was impossible to see the down-and-out's eyes, but he felt the heavy pressure of being watched and assessed; of being stripped clean right down to the bone. With a shiver he averted his eyes and lengthened his stride, quickly slipping down a side street to escape. It was the first time in his life that he had ever felt fear. He didn't like it one bit. In fact, it put the bloody willies up him.

CHAPTER III

He had given almost all of his adult life to the good works of Sant'Egidio. He believed the primary need of mankind was to have a home and shelter. Especially in a city. Without this basic requirement a man would lose himself; his sanity and his humanity. 'Whoever gives to the poor will not want...' In this city of God, there were 3,276 truly without shelter wandering the streets. Around 86% of them were men of which 24% were citizens of this land. He could recite all the statistics, but these figures could never paint the real picture of human suffering. Many were there after losing their means to meet the fiscal demands of city life and had made the choice of sorts, to make their home under bridges and along the river banks. For some, the step was intended to be temporary, but events had a way of holding onto you. Their shadowy lives were an open book for all to read. Most but not all.

'Did you see him?'

The words smoked their way between the threads of his thoughts, soft and sweet.

'Saw whom, bella?' Then. 'Yes, I saw him.'

'I was beginning to think that he had left or even worse, that we had lost him. It has been so long.'

'He knows how to disappear when he wants to. That's for sure.'

'Where does he go, you think and or even more importantly, how does he do it? Our city is small.'

'You must have noticed by now that he does not like us much. He avoids us. Only God knows why. He certainly doesn't use our Michelin guide. I have never seen such a loner.'

His companion, a short woman with broad hips and a kind, round, bespectacled face paired up at him. They had worked together now for many years and were comfortable with each other; brother and sister in God would be an apt description of their relationship.

'Nor the free barbershop and showers. He has been drifting around these streets long before I started working for the charity. I remember as a little girl catching the occasional glimpse of him as my parents drove me to early Sunday mass. I used to pretend that he was Michelangelo. In a way, I found his presence comforting. Do you think that strange, Franco?'

He chuckled. A rich, calm sound.

'Maybe he is and who am I to say what is strange. We don't even know his real name. He hasn't got any ID or papers. Not that I've ever seen, anyway. He is very mysterious, to say the least.'

'Have you ever managed to talk to him? He wouldn't let me get within five metres of him. Treats me like the plague. I'm not sure that he even has a voice.'

'Oh, he has a voice alright. It's profound and rumbles like brooding thunder from his chest.'

'How in heavens name do you know that, Franco? This

13

information may be valuable to add to his file. One day he will need us whether he likes it or not. They all do in the end.'

'I said he had a voice, but I didn't mean to imply that he has ever spoken to me.'

'If you don't stop being so evasive, I will kick you!'

He laughed again, but he seemed uneasy. Then he began hesitantly.

'About two years ago, I decided to take a cut through from the river. It was very late at night, and I was in a hurry to get home and against our rules, I was alone. As I passed the bundles of sleeping figures bathed in a yellow glow under the monumental colonnades of Jesus' first apostle, I heard the deepest voice in all the world muttering in a language that sounded vaguely Nordic. In a corner, propped up against the polished stone was a grey-bearded man whom I immediately recognised as our Gandalf. He appeared to be dreaming and was calling out in anguished tones. May God forgive me, I was curious and sat down next to him and held his hand. God punished me for intruding on an abandoned man's privacy for I learnt nothing new. However, after a short time, he grew calm. Up to that moment, I did not realise that he was missing an eye but his gaze on me that night now haunts me in my sleep. His pale blue eye was the colour of the sky on a bright winter's day when the frost lies heavy on the ground. Like in the clear mountains of Abruzzo at midday. It pierced my soul and pinned me to the wall.'

He crossed himself.

She stood silently for a moment studying his troubled face and instinctively understood that he was not his usual humorous self.

'What did he do?'

'Do? Nothing. He did nothing. He just watched me, like an eagle a mouse.'

'What did you do?'

'Me? I ran. Scuttled away like a sinner before the glory of God.'

'Your story has frightened me a bit, Franco. I hope for your sake you haven't made it up. If it's the truth, I'm sorry that I asked in the first place.'

He grinned mischievously at her and moved off.

'You have made it up, haven't you?' she said, punching him on the shoulder and laughing nervously.

'The words of a whisperer are like delicious morsels; they go down into the inner parts of the body. Which reminds me, don't we have a soup kitchen to open or do you prefer to gossip here all day?'

'You are a very strange man, Franco.'

'As I said earlier. Who am I to say what is strange.'

Despite the levity, they both wandered off guarding their own thoughts.

CHAPTER IV

Wandering a city, bereft of everything that marks you as human, is not an easy thing. Being invisible was not the issue, not worthy of anyone's notice, that was not the hard part. In fact, to many, it was the best part. No, what was worse is that those who are the nastiest or most thoughtless in society, saw you as an easy target for their shameful, basic and low actions; a blank canvas for them to paint their most base and darkest thoughts on. Thoughts that marked them out to be the real failures in life. These demons roamed about in many guises. Some wore uniforms, some were young, some not so young. Some were men, and some were women. Some had good jobs, and some had suffered what could only be called a challenging upbringing, acting out what had been done to them on others less fortunate in turn. Others still, had had everything that was possible to have, privileged beyond the expectations of most. What they all had in common, what tied them in the same black ribbon, was the emotional poverty they all shared. He had seen them all before and sometimes these learned things tumbled through his head, racing through the years, a kaleidoscope of fragmented images. Was this why the forgotten of the city unconsciously seek each other out? Why they tend to sleep and build their fragile shelters in the same areas? Huddled into a fraternity. Protection against those who thoughtlessly excluded them perhaps? They were lost, yes, but they still sought comfort from those in the shared wilderness. What was special about mankind was not his technical ability but his social adaptability. He observed everything for knowledge was the ultimate possession.

He sat in the chilled shadow of a bridge and watched the murky green water ripple by. Underneath its seemingly benign surface, he sensed its power and felt an unexplained kinship. Through its flow, he felt a link with a time he had long ago forgotten. If only he could jump into its depths and let it carry him backwards. Would that reawaken his memory? Or would such rashness be just a one-way journey beyond the veil? Disturbingly, both options were tempting. Somehow, he had a brief inkling that he had tried something like this before; another river, another age, another place. Or was it just the lingering essence of a fading dream? Whatever! It made no difference. His existence was now.

'Ahó, Greybeard! Catch any fish yet?'

The high voice followed by baiting laughter cut into his reverie.

'Don't eat anything from in there, Grandfather, otherwise you'll be shitting your pants before nightfall!'

He cocked his head like an eagle and fixed his eye, sky blue and clear, on the two heads leaning precariously over the bridge and silhouetted against the glare of the sun. He instantly recognised the boy from two weeks ago; the boy with quick hands. He gave a short wave of acknowledgement for good advice given, turning a blind eye to the intended mischief of it.

Something fell with a solid clinking sound by his folded knee.

'Buy yourself something fresh, Greybeard.'

The two heads immediately disappeared, and he returned to his wistful solitude, ignoring the small white purse with the black and red threads decorating its facade

 He lost track of time, but as greyness began to descend around the base of the bridge, he reached out a long-fingered hand and gently scooped up the purse and deftly opened it. Inside was a collection of one and two euro coins. He studied them for a while then tucked them away into his coat. An offering freely given and accepted is a thing of honour and draws the eye. He rose from his vigil by the river, lulled by the poetry of its rippling waters against the stones in the bank. He felt a vigour not experienced in a very long while. Something was pulling at him, and he felt compelled to follow it.

 He began to walk. The smooth cut stone of the walkway imprisoned between the high flood walls and the deceptively calm river felt hard and unrelenting under the worn soles of his leather boots. He never got tired, never felt cold, the heat did not touch him, and hunger was always a distant thing. They are thirty-five bridges over the ancient artery of this city, and he had walked under them countless times. He knew them intimately, what lay at the top of the steps rising to the platform of the living above, the realm where the blind and unaware chased the necessities of their daily existence and what lurked, hidden, alongside the river's banks. Every bridge was a punctuation to countless personal stories of people who had slipped and fallen from the city above. He passed isolated mattresses, some vacated, some jealously occupied. He passed what could only be described as outdoor dormitories. He passed covered lean-tos of cardboard mixed with plastic and tents with their tiny open-air kitchens tucked in next to them. He passed noisy gatherings of the new, undocumented arrivals either hiding jovially from the roving police or waiting to start a new wave of enterprise above. They all either pulled in or went silent as he drifted by. He was an outsider of the outsiders. It pleased him to be regarded in such a way. He had no urge to belong. Being among was good enough for him.

The city had ideas to reclaim these places for its citizens and paying visitors. He had seen the organised parties, standing out like a fly on a white wall, trotting along the walkways like garrulous geese, taking notes and making plans. It would eventually happen. The image of the city demanded it, and of course, the potential for coin grabbing was a great prospect. Scrubbed, cleaned and sterilised, then flooded with bright leisure, inviting and safe. Then where would the discarded go? Somewhere else. Always somewhere else, with their needles, litter, poverty, undiagnosed and untreated psychoses, and broken dreams. Never mind, the ingrained guilt of the Christians in this city of God will always find a place for them. Those who govern relied heavily on that.

On the face of the rough wall, black paint splashed in graphic and elegant depiction was the image of a raven about to take flight. Beak gaping and raucous. Wings spread wide. He stopped and studied it.

'I know you, bird! My memory, it will come back to me, and I shall know your name and where you have been.'

Then the stairway of stone pulled him upwards, his nostrils burning with the pungent, acrid smell of urine.

In a district where sailors, fishermen and slaves once lived uneasily side by side he made his way. These early inhabitants, long in their graves, would not be able to recognise the still

19

narrow twisting streets that used to tempt violence and fire for it was now a showplace of the modern city, shamelessly parading its interpretation of the old. However, in its now dark, cobbled streets he was able to slip by without drawing very much notice to his shabby, unwelcomed presence. It was here with its trendy bars, cat-walking tourist and drunken American college students, that he was being drawn. A binding had been made, and he was being called upon to play his part.

From the tantalising, shredded mists of memory, he knew that he almost always shared the pain and misery of those he dreamed about; everything else was lost. And so it was now in the waking world or was he somehow dream walking? He wasn't sure, but there was no turning back on this path. He felt the uncertainty, the racing elation of an animal in full flight, the desperation of certain entrapment, the denial of the odds, the brimming force of life and most of all, the courage to spit in the eye of the inevitable. His heart raced in unison with the object of his link, just like in his dreams, two but one. He was called, and he would answer as his son had done before the hammer of life had fallen from his hands. The son sometimes becomes the father by example. Change is wisdom; wisdom is change.

He watched, as if in slow motion, the slender, lithe boy turn to face the charging, yelling mob of wild-eyed thugs, bent on hurting what they hated but did not have the intellect to understand. In his dark, shining eyes there was no fear, just the pure exhilaration of the challenge. Heart to heart, strength to strength, courage to courage. He stepped into the space dividing them. The pack, secure in their numbers, skidded to a surprised halt. He just stood there, a dishevelled old man, observing them calmly from beneath his floppy hat, its edges pulled low over his face, forming an impenetrable shadow.

'What the fuck!' spat the leader. 'Get out of the way, you stinking hobo! Protecting your bum pal, are you? You dirty bastard!'

Their nasty words had no effect and echoed around the damp, narrow dead-end.

'Fuck this! Let's give the dirty, old bitch a kicking!'

With this they hurled themselves at him driven with the fury of their psychological frailty and fear, kicking and punching in a frenzy of mindless violence.

He felt the savage blows, numbing and painful, and fell under the onslaught, his head hitting the cobbles with a sharp, audible crack and rebounding, his scalp gashed and red. His flesh tore, and blood splattered darkly onto the street, mixing with the saliva from his drooling mouth. He did not struggle but absorbed the brutal beating in silence. He was dimly aware of the boy slipping away down a side lane, like an alley cat who knew how to survive, using every distraction as a boon. He did not feel disappointment, only insensibility and deadness. A bargain had been struck and accepted.

A sharp whistle, urgent and demanding, reverberated into the dampness, cutting through the brutality. The pounding of running boots following close after.

'Fermati! Fermati! Polizia!'

Heads were thrown up and legs, spinning on cowardly feet, swivelled and scattered into the darkness.

21

The pain and agony was a thing that pulsed with every fading beat of his heart, with every ragged breath through his bleeding mouth; his lungs wet and sucking with liquid. The voices floating down to him, disembodied, were not comforting.

'Poor bastard. They've done a real number on him. I don't think he'll make it.'

'Don't touch him, Enzo. He's crawling with lice. I'll call an ambulance.'

He felt a hard boot rolling him over and had no control over the groan that gushed from his mouth.

'Better give him a quick check, eh? Oh! What have we here? Santa Maria, it's filled with coins. Probably stolen. The poor bastard won't be needing this where he is going. God bless his soul.'

'Leave him alone, Enzo. The ambulance will be here soon. I don't think it will do him any good though. Look at the state of him! God have mercy! He's a bloody mess!'

They left him there lying on the hard, moist, uneven stones not even attempting to ease his suffering. He did not want or need their succour. He had endured much worse, but he couldn't recall what even when the puzzling image of a tree with deep roots anchored into the world flashed through his mind, and his missing eye began to itch annoyingly. Anyway, the pain held him fast and would not let him go. One thing at a time, one battle at a time. This is the way to win the war. Even if one was to perish in the end.

The ambulance arrived within ten minutes with a great flourish of speed, blue lights flashing. The paramedic hurried over to the fallen homeless man and assessed him in quickly and professionally.

'We know this one,' he said in a sombre tone. 'It's not the first time that he has been assaulted. He's tough as old leathe,r but this time it looks much more serious. I believe he has severe internal trauma.'

'Does he have any relatives or familiars that we can inform?' asked one of the policemen.

'No,' replied the medic. 'He is a born loner and a survivor. Been around for years. You may want to give Sant'Egidio a call though. Ask for Franco Valeri, he has some interest in Gandalf's case.'

'Gandalf?'

'Si. We don't know his real name. No papers and he does not speak. He looks a bit like the movie character, so that's what we call him.'

'Davvero? Okay, we'll make the call.'

'Grazie.'

Carefully transferred into a stretcher and gently strapped in, the old man was carried into the ambulance and whisked away with a blaring and honking siren making its presence known in the stillness of the night.

Late that night, sound asleep after another hard day doing his street rounds, Franco was harshly awakened by his mobile which he always kept on in case of emergencies. It was the police, not an unusual thing considering his type of clients. He immediately staggered out of bed, dressed, and drove to the nearby hospital in his battered, little electric, two-seater car.

Thankfully the Pronto Soccorso was quiet at this pre-dawn part of the night, and when he identified himself to the bored but smiling receptionist, it didn't take long for a doctor to come out to meet him.

'Buonasera, Franco,' she said. They had met on several other occasions in the past and were familiar with each other. 'Another one of yours, I assume?'

'Of a sort, Dottoressa. Not in the usual sense but I feel responsible for him. How is he?'

'You're a good man, Franco. He's not in good condition. We have him on an intravenous drip at the moment whilst we decide if he is strong enough to undergo surgery. We are also awaiting blood test on any chemical substances that he might have been using. He is a puzzle. He appears older than Methuselah, but his muscles are as hard as a rock. Do you know anything about him that might help us?'

'No, I'm afraid not, Doctor. He is an elusive creature and shies away from all human contact and offer of assistance. We know very little about his movements or habits accept that he has been on the streets of this city probably before either you and I were born.'

'How they survive out there I don't know,' said the Doctor with a faraway look in her eyes.

Franco didn't try to answer. Instead, he asked.

'May I see him, Doctor?'

'He's unconscious... ah, why not. The human brain is an unfathomable thing. Go on through. We have him in his own room, for now, but in the morning we will have to move him in with the others.'

Nodding his thanks, Franco pushed open the door and went in search of Gandalf.

On finding him, Franco was shocked. He had an oxygen mask on over his bearded face, and a drip ran down from a plastic bag on a stand through a tube and into the blue vein of his arm. His features were swollen beyond recognition and his bared chest was covered with bruises, purple, black and a sickly, jaundiced coloured yellow. This he had expected as he had seen it all too often before but what took him back was the unpredicted presence of the old man. He had expected to find a figure frail and shrunken, wavering on the edge of death. Instead, he saw a man with broad shoulders, sheathed in layers of hard, strong muscles. He looked like an athlete from his neck down to his covered waist. With a shake of his head, Franco took the elegant, long-fingered hand, the hand of an artist, despite the ingrained dirt, and held it in his broad hairy paw. He smiled to himself at the incongruous contrast.

'Don't you dare go to the bosom of our Lord before I learn your story, old fellow,' he whispered to the unconscious man. 'Besides, I don't think God has quite made up his mind on what to do with you as yet.'

He stood there for a long while listening to the faint, ragged breathing rasping from the open mouth of the old man. He had heard breathing like this before, and it signalled the fading of life.

He patted the finely veined hand and mentally said his goodbyes.

On the way out he saw the same doctor chatting to the receptionist. She glanced up as he approached and after one look at his face said.

'Not good, eh?'

'No, Doctor. Not good. Doctor...if the Almighty calls for him, please, would you do me a favour.'

'What's that.'

'Don't let a priest administer the last rites. It's something that he would appreciate.'

She looked at him puzzled but nodded, watching him as he made his way forlornly out under the green exit sign.

She stared out at the orange glow suffusing the near-empty car-park relaxing into this the quietest period of her shift which would come to an end at seven in the morning. Taking a deep breath, she went off to check on the results of her sole patient's blood test. Miraculously, it was negative on all counts, which was one step closer to clearing him for possible interventive surgery. She decided to go and check on her mysterious guest.

As she approached his room, a flustered nurse burst out into the corridor, a look of panic and concern in her eyes. The worse leapt into her mind.

'Doctor, he is gone!'

'Gone? What do you mean gone?'

She pushed past the shocked nurse and went to look for herself.

A rumpled empty bed gazed back at her, starched white with a splash of red blood on the pillow. It's occupant gone.

 Numbly she reached for her mobile and touched the number for Sant'Egidio.

CHAPTER V

He darted in. His right hand, palm covered by a piece of paper, punched, fingers extended, the button denoting 500 euros. Then he pulled back, looking relaxed unconcerned and disassociated. The middle-aged, expensively dressed woman, pressed frantically at the cancel button, desperately trying to undo what had so maliciously been done, distracted and suspended from her surroundings. Passer byes noticing her actions regarded the clean-cut boy standing nearby with suspicion but were unsure and indecisive. Then he struck again, superbly balanced and quick as a dancer. Lancing left, he pulled at her handbag, dangling by its strap on her left shoulder. As she swiftly grabbed at it to stay his thieving hand, he swivelled right, reaching around her and snatching a fistful of notes. She turned and screamed at him, dismayed by his audacity, but he walked away swiftly and nonchalantly. Witnesses to his theft moved in to protect the assaulted woman, but it was far too late.

Although it had been skillfully done, four-hundred euros for five seconds of work, there was no joy in it. Four nights ago an old hobo had saved him. 'The bastard. Why had he done such a thing? He didn't owe him nothing. Was it the bloody purse?' Snatched from a young mother distracted by her two brats almost as an afterthought. It meant nothing. Even little Nicu had thought him mad. The stupid imp.

'What you done, Tobar? You give money to a barbone! They beat you for sure.'

'Not if you keep your little trap shut, idiot! Anyway, it's my sodding money. I'll do what I want with it.'

And that was that. He was a bloody hero to the diminutive fool, and he would do anything for him. Clever bastard! He wanted him to teach him his tricks. Hero worship my arse! He had given the little leech the slip this morning. Couldn't stand his constant nattering. It was putting him off his work. Not as much as that blasted barbone though. They had given him a real kicking. Fuck! That could have been him. Bleeding all over the cobbles, he was. Dead for sure. That's what the thieving cops thought anyway. He had watched them on the sly. Bastards! Lifted the bloody purse from a dying man. Weren't they supposed to be the good ones? Two faced, thieving, musker bastards! And they said we didn't follow the rules of their hoity-toity culture. At least we didn't pretend. We are what we are. You don't want us, so we set our own standards. We won't lie down and disappear no matter how much you want us to. We will cling on to your balls for as long as it takes. You can't shake us loose no matter how much you hurt. Malign us as much as you like. We are here to stay. Look at how upset he has made me become! Why had he done that? Dirty Greybeard!

He had become a one-man crime wave. Bold as brass, vicious even. He pushed his chances aggressively right up to the limit, only backing down when the exchange of blows was imminent or overwhelming odds were against him. The polizia were now actively hunting him. He had become an embarrassment, him being a minor no longer the issue. More times than not he had had to run from them. The fat muskers! They couldn't keep up

29

with him. He was uncatchable. His controllers weren't happy either. Yes, he was bringing in more money than ever, but he was also turning the spotlight onto them. Threatening the organisation. Threatening their livelihood. 'Calm down, mate,' they said. 'Calm down or you'll bring the fucking roof tumbling on our heads!'

Despite his sour rancour, uncaring boldness and defiance he spread his hunting wider, avoiding his normal haunts, always on the move. Walking from early morning to late in the evening; footsore and angry. Guilt and self-recrimination rode his shoulder like a horse breaker rides a bucking bronco.

He was so absorbed in his mood that he saw them almost too late. As naturally as he could make it, he turned and started to cross the busy street. That's when they spotted him, immediately breaking into a run. He bolted. These were not the usual lazy stereotypes who ignored crime and civil disobedience right under their arrogant noses and gathered in companionable groups to gossip and quaff coffee, posing in their uniforms and lording it over the innocent. These belonged to a special unit. They were dressed in plain clothes. They were young, fit, highly trained and they knew him. Shit! He had gone up in the world. Somehow this did not reassure him. He ran with all the speed he could muster yet they were still gaining on him. Canny as an antelope, he slowed his pace, keeping the speedy predators in his periphery vision, then at the last moment, just as they were about to catch him, he turned sharply, twisting and spinning among the startled tourists and citizens. In the age-old primitive dance of prey and predator, he kept ahead of them, slipping from their grasping hands, evading their intent. More through luck than design, a car interposed itself between them, allowing him to race off down a crowded side street.

Lungs bursting he fled into a small, wooded park and collapsed against a tree, his head spinning and blood pumping.

'Shit, that was close!' he panted. 'Time to keep me head down. Bastard muskers got me cornered.'

He didn't dare take the tube home, for he knew they would have staked out the stations. By now, he guessed, they would have worked out where he was staying, his route and who his controllers were. The house of cards was about to fall, and his brazenness was the catalyst for it all. All because of that stupid Greybeard. Gave his bloody life for me. Cazzo! For the first time since his fourth birthday tears ran freely down his cheeks.

Exhaustion overtook him, and he curled up amongst the bushes and fell into fitful sleep, shivering uncontrollably in the middle of the night as the cold sought him out in his leafy refuge. His small back-pack, stuffed with money, clutched to his chest and stomach. It had now become a pillow, the only thing he possessed to give some degree of warmth and comfort.

He awoke in foggy, dripping dawn to birdsong, his eyes bleary and his face puffy, his clothes damp with moisture. Suddenly, the feeling of being not alone cleared his mind and raced his focus to the surface in a flush of self-preservation. A thing honed to sharpness by those of his kind, always hovering over the spinning sandstone wheel, keeping that fine edge. Living in and preying on a society that despised and wanted you gone was not a symbiosis made in heaven. Catholic guilt could only be stretched so far. The church and the state existed side by side along a thin, cosy line of expediency. A buffer zone could not always be relied upon. In the end, all that can save you is your wits.

 Staying very still even to the point of holding his breath, he allowed his eyes to swivel slowly in their crusted sockets, surveying inch by inch the world beyond his own personal thicket. There sitting with his back against the very tree on which he had collapsed after his narrow escape, was the bulky shadow of a man. He was as unmoving as the hard, rough trunk on which he rested, and he appeared entirely unaware of his presence in the bushes. Another small blessing. So far, so good. Now what? He watched the figure as the seconds and minutes ticked achingly by; unwilling to even blink. The blasted man sat there as if he intended to remain until the world came to an end. Bastard! His bladder began to call to him, distended and urgent. It could not be ignored, no matter how much he gritted his teeth and clamped his muscles, trembling all over with the effort. Just when he had decided to relax and let his dignity leak away, warm, wet and enticing, a voice as deep as a cavern, rumbled across to him.

'You had better go before you piss your pants, boy.'

He started and almost lost control of his sphincter. Shit! Then in the grey light, he saw the man more clearly.

'Santo cielo!' he thought. 'A bastard ghost!'

 He swiftly scampered out of the bushes and with nervous, fumbling fingers, freed himself in the nick of time before the gush of hot, yellow, steaming liquid cascaded noisily into the wet, organic humus at his feet. His head spun with ecstatic relief as he inhaled the pungent smell. Then he came back to his senses.

'Ahó, ain't you dead, mate?'

He did not receive an answer.

'Saw you face-planted and dead. You a ghost or what?'

The voice rolled in like thunder.

'I've been dead many times. Death is an illusion.'

The boy filled the space with silence.

'You're not one a dem useless uni profs, are yu? Waste of fucking time, them.'

Again, no answer was forthcoming.

'Glad you're not dead, mate.'

Silence.

'Why d'yu do it?'

'An offering was made and accepted.'

'Huh? Whatever. Thanks.'

'You are now being hunted. You must change and adapt.'

Then the greybeard rose to his feet and cast the boy in his shadow. He blinked in surprise. He had not expected this strange barbone to be so tall. His gaze was drawn to his one eye, and the sky opened, and he fell spiralling into it. He blinked again, and he found himself standing alone amongst the trees.

'By-the-way, my name's Tobar,' he muttered into the damp silence.

CHAPTER VI

When he received the news, he could not credit it. Sleep overtook him once again and brought him back down to a place of unconscious bliss. In the morning he started his worries and his enquiries. His first stop was the Polizia di Stato. It turned out that the assault on Gandalf the night before had not been reported in and therefore, did not exist in the records. Patiently, Franco explained what had happened and gave the name of the hospital and Doctor who had admitted and attended the victim. He could tell by the disinterested expression of the polizia interviewing him that nothing would be done. Who cared what happened to a rough sleeper? He then called a few contacts he had inside the Carabinieri. They were more sympathetic, took a thorough description of Gandalf, made a few humorous remarks, and promised to keep an eye out with no promises attached. Same old, same old. He had been down this path several times before. A little later than usual, he started his rounds. Here was where he would get the best results. Only those fallen or banished to the streets cared for or looked out for those like themselves. Everyone knew of Gandalf, but he had not yet met any who had ever spoken to him. However, he was a talisman to many. If he was still around then the world was still spinning, and there was hope of a kind for them. In a way, he was a sign of normality as he went about his business. Which of course, no one had an inkling of what that was.

He stopped to chat with a smiling old lady who had her hair perfectly groomed with every silver strand in its place. If it wasn't for the dirt coating it, her kindly face and her floral frock, she could have been anybody's carefree grandmother.

'How have you been keeping, Martha? Still have the best view on the river?'

She grinned happily and cackled. Her story was like many others. She had lived for years, a good housewife without any other aspirations, to a company director. One day he just walked out and disappeared without explanation. His small company, it later turned out, had collapsed into financial ruin and he had been overcome with the shame of failure. Martha waited and waited, preparing dinner for him every night. As she waited, the bills piled up. Her successful husband had handled everything. Her job had been to see to his every need. Finally, the eviction notice arrived, and although the courts had been sympathetic, the law was the law. Bewildered and lost, she found her way to the riverside where she slept for weeks under cardboard boxes and depended on the handouts of passer-byes as she sat at the top of the stairs. Her world consisted of a hundred metres of riverside. It was Gandalf who had built her a small shelter and provided her with a small stove and cooking utensils. With this small kindness, domestic normality returned to her, and she became the epitome of independence and self-reliance. Like her enigmatic benefactor no one had ever heard her speak but smiles and gestures aplenty she had.

'Want a cup of coffee?'

She nodded enthusiastically and although there was a coffee bar directly behind them neither glanced in that direction. Plain and simple, they did not serve the homeless, and they did not want them as they gave a bad impression. To whom was never clear.

He fished about in his backpack and produced a large flask and liberally poured a steaming cupful for her.

'Sugar?'

Again the smile and a nod, followed by two fingers shyly held aloft.

He dropped two cubes into the brown, fragrant liquid, gave it a stir and handed it to her. She sipped at it with an elegant flair.

'Seen Gandalf lately?' he asked after a while.

Her sparkling grey eyes immediately became dull with sadness, and she lay her cheek against her open palm and closed her eyes.

'No, Martha. He's alive. If you see him, will you let me know?'

She nodded, her eyes dancing once again and continued sipping her coffee.

It was mostly like this with everyone that he spoke to. Gandalf had done his disappearing trick again. What intrigued him more than anything, was how an old man, beaten to within an inch of his life and hovering at death's door could get up and walk out of a hospital without anyone seeing him and vanish into a modern city without a trace. If for no other reason, he had to find him to get the answer to that one. He only hoped that he wasn't in fact, lying dead in the bushes of a derelict park somewhere.

As he was walking back, sunk deep in thought -dodging the crowds of tourist streaming in both directions along the pedestrianized giant thoroughfare carved by a dictator in past times- when he noticed a young, lithe, Romani boy of about twelve years, casually helping himself to the wallets and purses of the awed sightseers. He did it in such a smooth, skilful and relaxed way that no one seemed to have noticed and those who did, thought perhaps that maybe they had been mistaken. He followed the boy's disturbing exploits as he carried out his sleight of hand performance under the ponderous observation of the impressive stone bowl of death. What was, continues to be. 'So whatever you wish that others would do to you, do also to them, for this is the Law and the Prophets.'

A duo of strolling polizia spotted his illicit activities and yelled across to the highly gifted thief. He waved cheekily to them, grinning impishly before slipping into the constantly shifting crowd like a seal diving into the rolling waves of the sea to avoid a predator. The guardians of the law strolled on, reluctant to disturb their bella figura.

He understood the stance of these much-maligned people, but in the same breath, he could not say that he agreed with their actions. He remembered the words of an unnamed police chief. He proposed that a simple solution was to expel Romania from the EU. That he admitted, was not possible, but the problem was not that decent society was racist. It was they who did not know how to behave in modern western society! The Romani culture was patriarchal he alleged, and the men had no concept of work. They would play cards in their despicable and unhygienic camps all day and send their women and children out to work. This work, unfortunately, meant begging and thieving. They knew no better.

This man lacked a historical perspective in his opinion. Some of his words were dangerously true, and people who were too lazy or too afraid to look further would immediately lap them up and vomit back their misunderstandings with vehemence and hatred. As he understood it, the Romani originated somewhere in Northern India where they were skilled metal workers. As it was in times of war, they were invited into Europe by men restless for territory and power, to assist in the building of canons. Their difference and closed knit culture, now that their task was done, discouraged the indigenous population from allowing them to integrate. Prohibited from owning property they had to take to the life of the wanderer in order to survive. Under the mistaken belief that these newcomers were from Egypt, the name Gypsies was born. What do a people do to make ends meet when they find themselves excluded from what others consider commonplace? They pulled in on their ancient skills, becoming tinkers and pot menders. They became famous for their love of dancing and music. They became fiercely protective of what was theirs and continued the age-old traditions of kin and tribe. However, everyone and everything outside of this circle was fair game. All in the name of survival of culture. As a devout Christian he wanted to help, but most times he just did not know how so he concentrated his efforts on the homeless. This boy demonstrated the clear struggle that he carried inside his spirit; a dichotomy he was unable to come to terms with. The words of a well-meaning, elderly citizen after the forced clearance of a camp always haunted him, 'They should be killed, but we cannot kill them.' May God have mercy on his soul for voicing such a terrible thing.

CHAPTER VII

He spent the rest of that day and the next, hiding and running from everybody, the police, his controllers, his new family, all the world that he once knew. He had joined the ranks of the homeless. Great! Another step up in the world. Wasn't that against the international law of human rights standards or something? He had a bag full of money and nowhere to go. He avoided everything from his past. Old Greybeard's advice was sound, but there was nothing there that he didn't already know. He wasn't born yesterday. He was bored stiff, and he missed the showers and clean clothes that he had grown accustomed to. He also missed talking to people. He was good at talking. He had a quick tongue, his controllers had been fond of saying. 'Careful it doesn't earn you a slap, though.' Blow them! By now the muskers would have rumbled their cosy nest. Serve them right! Greedy bastards!

He wanted to find that bloody dead man who had risen up again like a bloody modern day Jesus Christ. If he had had anyone to tell his story to, they would have laughed at him and told him to stop doing drugs. He didn't do that shit. Never did. He knew what he had seen and heard. It was that shifty Greybeard for sure. Where in hell's name had he gotten to? An old geezer like that couldn't just disappear! He found himself slinking along all the well-known hot spots where the homeless tend to congregate. It was safe enough as the muskers rarely go among them unless they had someone to arrest because of a murder or something. 'If you don't see it, it ain't happening.' Convenient policy if you ask me. Anyway, nobody ever bothered to ask his opinion even though he had them aplenty.

Nighttime found him tired and weary of spirit. He curled up in an as yet unclaimed corner and tried to sleep. His stomach was nicely full as he certainly wasn't short of money. However, even the homeless didn't want him around. They saw who he was, 'a dirty Zingari' and was suspicious of his intentions. A man could find prejudice even in the deepest hole. Maybe they had a point though. His people had a bad reputation for thieving. These folk had very little left to call their own, and they didn't want that lifted while they slept. Whatever! It was their problem. Let them deal with it. He just wanted a place to sleep free from the spiteful muskers. Firmly planting his head on his bag he wrapped his arms tightly around it, hugging it to his chest and promptly fell asleep.

Sometime in the middle of the night, he was awakened by a very gentle tugging motion. He sat up, quick as a snake with his little knife which he always carried, waving about in front of his face. In the near pitch darkness of his corner, he caught a glimpse of what appeared to be an old lady skittering away like a squirrel back into the uncertain light. 'Thieving bitch!' he muttered and went back to sleep.

As usual, he woke up just after dawn, shivering and bleary-eyed. To his surprise, someone had dropped an old, threadbare blanket beside him. Although it wasn't the cleanest, beggars can't be choosers, came to mind. Fine time to have a laugh, eh? He wrapped the blanket around him, head and all, and listened to the river. The world down here felt peaceful, and someone had given him a fortune during the night. Although it was worth keeping in mind that someone else had almost stolen one from him. It made him wonder. Was it perhaps the same person, carrying out some strange idea of fair barter? It left him with a guilty feeling.

Some couple of hours later when the river denizens began to stir, a little, smiling old lady in a floral dress sidled up to him and delicately placed a cup of hot water by his drawn up feet. Without a word, she turned and disappeared under the nearby bridge from which she had come. He eyed it suspiciously but after a pause, stuck his hand out, picked it up and sipped the steaming liquid. It was delicious.

Odd characters of every shape and type were now up and wandering about, engaged in the rituals of their daily lives to which he couldn't quite make out the point. They all ignored him but then again, they did not glare suspiciously at him as they had done the evening before. He assumed that they had all woken up with their meagre possessions where they had left them so in their minds, he had passed the test. Wonderful! Welcome to the community of the hopeless. Stupid buggers! Now he had to find a place to piss.

Under the cover of his borrowed blanket, he squished a twenty euro note into his empty cup and having done so, folded the blanket as neatly as he could, then walked off in the direction of the bridge. At the far end, he saw a sturdy, patchwork, little shelter with the old girl busily boiling an egg. As he passed he smoothly bent down and placed the folded blanket with the cup balanced on it next to her. She looked up into his eyes and smiled. Neither said anything. He continued on his way.

41

He spent the day exploring the riverfront, something he had never had the time to do before, emerging now and again to buy prosciutto sandwiches and coke from a mobile street stall. The vendor couldn't care less who he was once he paid for his purchases up front.

Late that evening he drifted back to where he had started feeling inexplicably free and content. As he passed the floral bird's house, it appeared deserted although there was now a lot of activity by the river. He placed some wrapped sandwiches by her small kitchen cooker and headed for his corner. It was still untaken except for his threadbare blanket, which had found its way back to him like a lost puppy, and a couple of flattened cardboard boxes with a blue plastic cover completing the package. He immediately laid down on the cardboard, wrapped the blanket around his thin frame and pulled the plastic over it all. 'Home, mother,' he whispered to himself.

He and Flora, as he now called her, developed a silent understanding of friendship. In a way, they had adopted each other. With the money he was slipping her she began to bring back better food and spent a lot of time cooking now that she could afford more fuel for her little stove. If the others noticed they didn't let on, but many gave him and his ever-present bag, odd glances. He became the primary beneficiary of her culinary skills, but she was also generous with those who had always been around her. Everyone accepted her largesse graciously and tried to do things in turn to help her, but she was one of those people who needed very little to be content.

One drizzly morning, a tall, dark-haired man with deep kind eyes and an easy way about him drifted down the stairs. He called out to everyone he met by their names, and they all seemed genuinely happy to see him, and many went over to greet and chat with him. Tobar was sitting with Flora helping her to clean her few dishes after having had a delicious meal when he casually strolled over.

'Ciao, Martha,' he greeted, his voice warm and rich. 'Any news yet?'

 She shook her head and smilingly handed him up a cup of coffee. He took it without hesitation or judgement.

'Oh, thank you,' he said with real pleasure and took a sip. 'I needed that.'

 Then his eyes fell softly on Tobar.

'Who's your new friend, Martha? He looks a fine lad. My name is Franco, young man. I too count myself a friend to Martha. She is the best of all women.'

 He held out his hand, but Tobar did not take it.

 The man called Franco did not seem offended in the least and continued smoothly.

'You two take care of each other. There is a lot of rain forecast for next week. It's coming down from the north where it has been wreaking havoc.'

 With that, he returned the empty cup to Martha and with a wave of his hand and a 'Hope to see you both again soon,' continued on his way, chatting to all as he went.

 Those two weeks spent by the river were the best two weeks of his entire life. He belonged to a community of the lost, of the mad, of the forgotten but each and every one of them had a measure of gold in their hearts. For the first time in his life, he belonged. People will give all of what they possessed, a blanket, a cup, a dented kettle, whatever, knowing that someone, in turn, will help them make it to the next day. They all lived separately, but strangely, they were more together than any community he had ever seen. And Flora? She was the greatest treasure of all. She was something that he had only had in his childhood dreams. That lonely part of him that had never been filled was slowly drawing in warmth. He was gradually being allowed to become human. No one demanded anything from him but gave without asking and accepted without looking to offer payment. Then, as warned, the rains came.

They had all been expecting it, but the suddenness and the elemental force of it took them all by surprise. And worse of all, it came in the dead of night.

The weather had been heavy during the entire day, the black clouds brooding and threatening the city with its bad mood. The city above went about its business in the usual fashion, for city dwellers have very little respect for the awesome power of the gods. Night is banished by the eternal glow of electricity. Weather and the rigours of travel put on hold by the availability and comfort of the motor car. Buildings of steel and concrete provide lifelong security and protection. Those without access to these things remember the fears of their ancestors and pay attention. Slowly and mechanically the people thanked the river for hosting them and went about packing and gathering their few belongings. They waited all day fatalistically, but nothing happened. They were reluctant to depart before it was absolutely necessary for them to leave for they had nowhere else to go. Through it all,

Martha kept smiling and Tobar held on to his courage because of her smile. Uncertainty had found him again, but this time he did not feel alone. They all went to their rudimentary beds thinking that maybe things weren't that bad after all and tomorrow was another day. Then the clouds burst, venting their fury down on the heads of mankind.

Caught at their lowest ebb, their hope rudely disrupted, the community of the homeless huddled together under the bridges like herding bovines. They knew better than this, yet were not acting on their knowledge, waiting for a herdsman to show them the way.

'We should go,' shouted Tobar to a concerned looking Martha. She was no longer smiling, but she smiled down at him.

Just when he was thinking to haul her away nevertheless, a group of florescent garbed civil volunteers, bright torches shining agitated beams of anxiety, bustled down the stone stairs shouting urgently at the huddled and indecisive community.

'Common, vai, vai! Vai su! Leave your things! Go now!'

Galvanised into sudden movement, they surged forward, crowding through the torrential rain and up the steep, narrow stairway, dragging their soaked bundles after them against all advice.

Half-way up the slippery stairs, Martha pulled away, pushing and clawing back the way she had come.

'No!' shouted Tobar but instinctively followed after her.

At the bottom, he caught up with her and pulled her to a halt.

45

She looked at him with a frightened and anxious face, silently imploring him. He knew what she wanted. Her prized cooker. He nodded his head vigorously and pointed firmly back to the stairs.

'Go, Go! I'll get it!'

Then he darted off, surprised at the now violent speed and rush of the river which was already gushing its rising waters up onto the walkway. He was out of his element, and he knew it, but a promise is a promise. Suffused from head to toe with nervous energy and speed Tobar grabbed the little cooker and sprinted for the stairs. He could no longer see the stone of the walkway due to the madly flowing water and misjudged his footing. Before the horrified eyes of the gesticulating and yelling volunteers, his right leg plunged over the lip, and the merciless river wrenched him into her grasp with an undertow of incredible strength. The last thing they saw was his thin arms flying into the air and the cooker spiralling away. Then he was gone. They stared in shocked disbelief and Martha screamed. Anguish so profound that they were all frozen in time and place.

Tobar had never experienced such a mighty power before; an overwhelming natural force of incomprehensible proportions and magnitude. He was nothing, insignificant, engulfed, his mind suspended in shock. The unstoppable hand of mother nature was bearing him away. He was the price she demanded for her bounty. To struggle against her was futile. Still, he strived for life, and as something hard and heavy crashed resoundingly into his ribs at a tremendous velocity, his arm flew out instinctively and wrapped around it. A tree trunk sent by Christ to save him. '...so he stretched out his hand and caught it, and it became a staff in his hand...' Bloody hell! Then the river plunged and plummeted him down into its dark depths in one breath and heaved him up into the air with another, spinning him like a useless doll. He no longer felt his body. It was numb and belonged somewhere else. The tumultuous water was so cold, leaching what was left of his warmth from his core. His spirit, tethered by a thin fading cord of mist hovered over his near corpse as it clung to life and a branch. Then as fierce lightning split the sky down its middle, a blinding, dancing, white light, jagged and terrible, he saw a vision. A lone man, long grey hair and beard blowing furiously in the wind, tearing through the rain and the madly raging torrent. His feet splashing, throwing up an unbelievable spray with the speed of his long legs. Unbelievably keeping pace with his one-way dash to a watery grave. Each time the lightning cleaved the darkness with its searing knife of light, this unlikely vision would reappear. 'No fucker can run that fast! Even looks like bloody Greybeard. Crazy bastard! Ain't right in the head!' was his irreverent thought. He fixed his eyes on the madcap storm runner as a dying man fastens onto the image of an angel coming to collect his soul. The crashing of thunder and the roaring river crushing down on his senses. Then the vast, spiteful current found a different way to torment him. With a tremendous surge of elemental power, it hurtled him towards the apparition to show him the falseness of hope before he died. Then in a fit of vindictiveness, it smashed his puny little body into the unforgiving wall to deliver the cruel coup de gras. The hand of a god, arm banded in rods of iron, seized him and yanked him upwards into descending blackness. 'This is it then. Fuck!' His last thought faded into nothing as the stygian curtain fell.

CHAPTER VIII

Franco and Rosaria, his long-time friend and work colleague, had just exited the Comunità di Sant'Egidio after a refreshing late night prayer session followed by discussions when the heavens opened up. Even by racing across to her nearby parked off-roader they were drenched to the skin before they could climb into its leather upholstered interior.

'This is bad,' observed Franco. 'I knew it was coming but didn't expect such a deluge. It's truly biblical!'

'Well, this isn't your ark. Shall I drive you home?'

'No, take me to our community on the river. They will be in need of help tonight by the look of things.'

'No rest for the wicked,' she grumbled good-naturedly and turned the ignition key.

Purring throatily, the top of the range vehicle rolled smoothly through the now flooded streets.

Franco was worried. Especially for Martha and others like her. Now she appeared to be attempting to build something she had lost. Something she had never had. The Romani boy was suspiciously familiar. He couldn't place why but eventually it would come to him. However, laying that aside, he had no place being amongst these vulnerable adults. They were kindly in many respects, but they also carried the scars of great imperfections. He was a minor and should be adequately cared for. How had he ended up there? His story hinted of great personal tragedy as the Romani cared jealously for their own. Family ties, despite the unfamiliar knots that bonded them, were strong and tight. Still, for some reason, he had not filed a report; had remained silent.

The rain was plummeting down so hard now that despite the frantically whirring windscreen wipers, visibility was almost nonexistent. However, this city was theirs. They were born and bred here and could find their way around blindfolded; well almost. As they pulled up in the street running alongside the river, they spotted a collection of white tents with civil volunteers in bright yellow, high-vis, waterproofed jackets and overalls running between them from one to the other; dipping in and out on urgent errands of some sort. Most disturbing of all was the presence of an ambulance.

'Looks like the cavalry has already arrived,' commented Rosaria. 'We had better go and see what's going on.'

Inside the white awnings was a bleak and subdued atmosphere. A collection of the riverside community stood around looking wet, trapped and dull-eyed. They were all staring uncertainly at the medics working over a small body strapped into a stretcher. Cowering in a far corner was the bedraggled and weeping figure of Martha. Franco immediately started towards her but stopped as a familiar voice called out to him. It was the coordinator of the volunteers from this sector. A very old acquaintance. His round, unshaven face was dripping moisture, and his red-rimmed eyes seemed haunted.

'Franco, do you know that boy? He's obviously Romani but when I asked these folks none of them had anything to say. What was he doing here, Franco? He's a minor…'

'What happened here, Nicola?'

 The troubled-looking man wiped his face with a pudgy hand and looked out through the half-open flap at the blinding sheet of water cascading down relentlessly. A deafening clap of thunder directly overhead made them all jump. It sounded as if the very sky was falling down on their heads.

'It shouldn't have been possible, Franco.'

'What, Nicola? What shouldn't have been possible?'

'The water was up to his chest. Even the riverboats had broken away from their moorings and were breaking apart on the bridge, but still, he walked through it. Never seen such a thing before, Franco. Waded uphill through the impossible! No one could bloody well stand in that current much less walk against it. Not possible, Franco. Not possible.'

'Who? Who did this, Nicola?'

'Had the boy over his shoulder. Just like bloody St Christopher. Forgive me, Lord!' he said, crossing himself. 'Must have pulled him from the river. Only God knows how. It shouldn't have been possible, Franco.'

'What's he talking about, Franco?' whispered Rosaria in his ear. 'Did the boy fall in the river?'

 He frowned down at her but didn't reply.

'Who rescued the boy, Nicola? Who was this man?'

'Looked like bloody Moses! Long grey hair and beard. Handed the boy over and bloody disappeared. Didn't say a word. It shouldn't have been possible, Franco! Not bloody possible!'

Franco felt a coldness spread along his body that had nothing to do with the inclement weather.

'Is the boy okay?' he found himself asking.

'Yeah, he's fine. Knocked about but fine. Pumped a bit of river water out of him. Tough as nails these Romani kids.'

'And the man?'

'Gone, I tell you, Franco! Bloody gone!'

Franco glanced across at Martha. It wasn't yet the time to talk to her but he felt an urgency to do so.

CHAPTER IX

He stood under a gnarled, thick-trunked, oak tree feeling its vast age as it breathed ever so slowly against his back. The electricity in the air shimmered against his skin, and the fine hairs on his arms rose up despite the wet. He had dreamt of that boy again but other than vague recollections, he could remember very little of it. Thunder. Where are you boy? Death cannot hold you forever. Lightning, rain, and that terrible serpent, wet, slimy and powerful. He felt somehow that he knew that worm and it wanted to devour the boy purely to spite him. He would have none of it. 'I will pierce you with Gungnir, the swaying one, sharp and true, and rip out your innards!' He felt anger rising in him and thought that the lightning flashed more violently in time with it. Foolish! He was growing foolish in old age. Dotage is the punishment for pride among mere mortals. Now, where did that come from? 'How I rue the day that I accepted that offering thrown from that bridge of light. The dreams, even here in the house of he who smote me, are becoming more vivid and troublesome. Something had to be done, but what? 'Memory, where have you flown off to? I need you now more than ever. Thought is all I have, but he is elusive and unreliable.' He turned his gaze to the dark branches above his head and imagined a shifting shadow in its depths and a flutter of wet feathers.

A man and a woman, drunk on sweet wine, ran blindly through the pouring rain with a tattered umbrella held aloft, laughing with lowered inhibitions and panting from the heady exertion of the unusual. As they entered the grove of his leafy shelter, they saw him and skidded to a halt.

'Cazzo! Un barbone!' his alcoholic breath steaming in the damp air.

He pulled on the laughing woman's arm, and they ran off again. She turned her head over her shoulder and shouted.

'Schifo!'

He watched them and saw their future as a searing flash of lightning tore the sky, illuminating the distant line of trees and buildings in a dull, fluorescent silhouette. He closed his eye and banished the omen.

The welfare of the boy, resolute and fierce in the face of danger, still pulled at him. He was a bright flame, burning all the fuel within his small body indiscriminately. He belonged to the time of heroes, to the time when the old gods ruled, not to this era when men and women were confused as to their purpose. When their only abiding drive was to hold on to life until nothing was left of mind and vigour. A drooling husk, mumbling and shuffling about with indignity. A time stifled by unjust laws where a man was not allowed to protect himself or his kin without fear of incarceration. This boy had no fear and did what he thought was right, whether it be wrong or not.

He lurched forward, his limbs feeling ponderous and heavy as if he was still yet to recover from a great exertion. Something he had been thinking about just three seconds hence but now had been washed away down the broken drain with the rushing water. He felt disconnected as if he were walking in several places at once. A flash of lightning, like a spear seeking his flesh, seared through the darkness, stabbing relentlessly into the earth in a frustrated frenzy. He staggered from its onslaught and the iron jaws of darkness, wolf cloaked, seeing his distraction, closed in, crushing his neck, driving him to his knees. He shook his head trying to throw the heavy weight from his back. As his vision cleared he focused on the orange glow of the gushing water as it flowed over his hands. Man's fear of his shadow has led him to create the perpetual day. A thing that not even the gods could do for it was against the laws of the world tree that binds all things. With a heave, he pushed himself back to his feet. How had he fallen so easily on his hands and knees in this alien city? The past, the present, and the future. Which was it? The price of an eye. It was making him dizzy. Oh, the pain of it! He couldn't afford to linger here much longer. The eastern God was closing in on him once again, but he couldn't leave yet. A young devotee, born out of his time, needed him for a little while longer. Weaving this way and that on trembling, unsteady legs, he side pedalled into the wide, open, rain-drenched street. Out of nowhere, two beams of light cut their way through the sheeting torrent and fixed themselves on him. Ensnared, he thrashed about violently, overbalancing and falling once again onto the flooded asphalt. A four by four slewed crossways behind him, antilock brakes engaging in the nick of time, stopping just five feet from his fallen body. His soul was in another world, and the sky was on fire. He could no longer centre his consciousness surrounded as he was by the breaking of the worlds. Was he reliving the past or seeing the future? Or was it just pure madness, destroying him from within?

He could feel the steady, well-meaning arms helping him back up onto his feet. Son? He had had many of them. Not all will survive, but even the prophecies can get it wrong. He was the living proof of that. Maybe.

'Let me help you. Let me help you.'

 The words were warm and soft, but he was not the one in need of succour. He was born to endure till the end of time. Still, an ally is an ally.

'What's wrong with him? Is he drunk?'

'Shush, no. Not drunk. Help me get him in the car.'

'You've just earned yourself a valeting job tomorrow,' there was no spite in the voice, just humour, used to hide uncertainty.

 Inside the belly of the beast, he felt warm and comfortable. His strength too had begun to return to him as it had done in the past. He remained unmoving and bided his time, listening to the rush of the world as it spun on in darkness.

'What shall we do with him, Franco? Take him to a shelter?'

'Certainly not! And besides, they will all be full by now. Especially on a night like this.'

'What then, my good Samaritan?'

 After a long pause, the answer came.

'We'll take him to my apartment. At least until tomorrow.'

'What! That's against all the rules, Franco. It's your funeral but don't you dare ask me to wash his clothes.'

 The humour again. The concern for a friend. Sometimes one

needed to look beyond the words to find true meaning.

'No. I wouldn't think of it, but I would like you to give him a shave.'

Her spontaneous laugh was filled with affection. It helped him to pull his mind together.

'Will he be alright, you think?'

'Yes, there are many things odd about this man, but weakness is not one of them. In fact, it is his strength that I'm worried about.'

'St Christopher, eh?'

'No, not him. Something else.'

She glanced at him, questions brimming in her eyes.

'Later, Rosaria. Let's talk later.'

Twenty minutes of driving through an abandoned city that appeared to be drowning in a concrete lake, they arrived at the Venetian styled apartment block where Franco lived. They found their elderly passenger fast asleep and nothing they could do would rouse him to complete wakefulness. Together they manhandled him out of the car, and half walked, half dragged him through the drenched but ornate courtyard, up the stairs and awkwardly between the obstinately shutting front door. He seemed to be extraordinarily heavy as if his bones were made from lead and by the time they managed to get him to the lift, they were sweating and panting despite the chill of the night.

'My God! There will be a reckoning for this, Franco,' muttered Rosaria darkly, the glasses on her round face misting up.

He smiled at the owl-like image.

They reeled out of the lift on the fourth floor and crashed to the pavement in an untidy heap, but even this did not disturb their now snoring guest.

'Are you sure he isn't drunk? Reminds me of my grandfather,' panted Rosaria. 'He was a drunken bastard!'

'Rosaria!' admonished Franco.

'Sorry, God,' she muttered. 'It's his fault.'

Franco wasn't sure as to whose feet she was laying the blame.

Together they plopped the dead weight of Gandalf on the sofa and sat down on the floor to watch him.

'He does pong a bit,' said Rosaria.

'Could have been worse,' agreed Franco. 'River water and rain have scoured him clean.'

'Really! I hadn't noticed.'

Outside the storm had intensified, if that were possible, and the rain was hammering on the window.

'Have you noticed that there isn't a mark on him?'

'I did notice. Last time I saw him, he was lying almost dead in a hospital bed.'

They stood there gazing at the sleeping man.

'There's a spare room,' said Franco.

'I have a reputation to protect, you know. May I have a shower?'

'Be my guest.'

'Well, I hope you serve a good breakfast. You'll have two hungry mouths in the morning without a doubt.'

With that, she crawled to her feet with a groan and headed for the shower.

CHAPTER X

Tobar opened his eyes to the ugliest woman he had ever seen.

'So this is what death is,' he thought.

Then the woman smiled, and things got much worse.

'Oh, you're finally awake, my handsome man. Been for a swim in the river I hear. Lots of germs in there, you know,' she said, bending low and dropping her voice conspiratorially. 'We had to pump you full with antibiotics. Nasty creatures, river germs.'

He stared at her, unable to take his eyes away.

'Are you hungry? I'll sneak something in for you. Men are always hungry in my experience.'

Against his will, he nodded slightly.

'Right you are then. I'll be right back. Try not to make too much noise. We don't want anyone spoiling our fun. Doctors are not known for their sense of humour. Pompous arses, the lot of them.'

Then she was gone.

He seized the opportunity, sat up quickly in bed, maybe a little too soon as the room span a bit, and had a look around his prison cell. A hospital then and the bloody storm was still blowing up a racket outside by the sound of it. He didn't like hospitals. Not that he had ever been in one before but still, he didn't like the sound of them. People went there to die, and it is well known that these places belong to the state which made them even worse. The state was nasty, just like those germs, and two-faced. He had to get out fast, but he was hungry and ever so tired. Where was Signora Ugly-face anyway? How long did it take to get a plate of food?

Just as he was thinking to check out the lay of the land to engineer his escape, the beauty whisked back through the door. Her knowing eyes gave him a glance, and she smiled again, pressing her index finger over her lips. What noise could he possibly make lying flat out on a bed anyway? However, his attention was caught by the little box in her hand, and his eyes followed it like a cat a mouse. She smiled again. 'God! I wish she wouldn't do that!' he thought. 'I just want to eat.'

As if hearing his thoughts she bustled over and opened the box cover with a flourish. Inside was a neatly packed hamburger, and it smelled delicious. Where did she get that from? He suspected that she was a mid-night snacker and this was her treat for tonight's shift. His mouth started to water. She noticed his anticipation and smiled yet again. 'Shit!'

'Here you are, little man. Don't gulp it down in one go. Take your time and chew slowly. Can't be bothered to be cleaning up sick at this time of night.'

He ignored her advice and although he felt a bit queasy after his fourth bite, he took a deep breath and dived in again. He didn't throw up. Romani kids don't throw up good food. They were much stronger than namby-pamby city apron-string kids. Bloody weaklings!

'Well done! You are a man of passion, I can see.'

He gave her a little smile, lay back on his pillow, closed his eyes and pretended to go back to sleep. She wasn't a woman easily fooled it appeared as although she didn't disturb him, she remained by his bedside like a guard dog. Who the hell was she? She wasn't one of them sour nurses from what he could tell. He never got an answer for his pretence soon became a reality, and he fell into sleep.

They came for him at mid-morning the next day. The storm had blown over, and the sun was shining as if nothing untoward had happened. A prim, elegantly dressed, polite woman in tight trousers that revealed everything whilst concealing everything accompanied by a smiling policewoman in a well-pressed uniform, appeared at his bedside. He wasn't taken in by their sunny disposition. He knew their dark intent. Bastard state flunkies! He looked around for support from Signora Ugly-face, but she was long gone and nowhere to be seen. Typical. 'I don't need nobody anyway!' Still, he thought it would have been nice to say a 'thank you' and 'goodbye'. They watched him getting dressed like a hawk watches a lizard. 'Ain't a man allowed a little modesty these days!'

Miss tight arse, and he meant that literally, was from the social services and he had spent the night in a particular hospital for minors, she informed him in a sultry voice used to disguise disinterest. She was a social worker, and they were taking him to a nice centre that will be his home for a while. She thought that he would like it there. Silly lying bitch!

They took him to a reasonably large building which had two burly security men at the locked reception.

'These nice men are here to protect you, Tobar.'

Yeah, right and his first name was idiot.

The place was crawling with sly looking kids from about six to his age, all involved with some type of chore overseen by a bunch of young men and women. It all looked a bit too familiar for him.

He played the game that was expected of him for a couple of weeks. He became the model inmate with an impeccable attitude, winning his way into the souls of the carers and at the same time, staying clear of the back room infighting amongst the other children. He observed and, clocked everything. Old Greybeard hadn't fished him from certain death for him to languish in a modern day workhouse. No, the old bastard wouldn't have risked his life for that. That man was like a mountain. Nothing could overcome him. Well, nothing will stop him either. He took to chatting with the two guards who rebuffed him at first but soon they began to smile at his dirty jokes about the tight-trousered social worker who had brought him here. They both had hidden their lust for her curvy body under a thin veil of professionality. But he had peeled that away with the sharp edge of his profane wit and provided an avenue for them to live out their forbidden fantasies under the guise of harmless humour. He knew them well for what they were and played them like a true master.

On that final evening of his captivity, he saw an opportunity and took it. He had stopped off, as usual, to chat with the two bored guards, regaling them with imaginative but false bits of gossip concerning the object of their special interest. They knew that he was making it all up but couldn't help themselves with the illicit visions he was creating in their base imagination.

'Oh, here she comes now! Watch this.'

Before they could think to stop him, he slipped by them and stood by the sealed glass door with a big smile of greeting painted on his impish face. Coming towards the entrance was Miss Tight-pants herself with a little girl in tow. The poor captive had an expression of utter distress and appeared inconsolable, clinging to her warden's leg in search of some type of comfort. As the electronic latch was released by the guards, Tobar stepped forward boldly and cooed.

'Oh, what have we here? Aren't you a beautiful bambola!'

The little girl's reaction was to immediately shy away, gripping even more tenaciously to the social worker's leg, causing her to stop halfway through the open door and attempt to disentangle the little girl as gently as possible. Of course, Tobar moved to hold open the door even more widely for her, a natural and courteous thing to do. As the woman and girl shuffled awkwardly into the hallway, only Tobar was left standing in the empty, yawning doorway with nothing but air separating him from liberty. Without a sign of warning, hesitation or a backward glance he bolted for it like a cat out of a bag. Everyone was dumbfounded and stared after him non-pulsed. Before the guards realised that they had been duped and could galvanise themselves, he was long gone.

'Don't just stand there, idiots! Catch him!' was the last thing he heard as he dived and dodged through the city's traffic, the smell of pollution in his nostrils and the wind of freedom in his hair.

CHAPTER XI

The shaking sound grew like a strong wind coming. He heard it. He felt it. His bed was shaking, startling him to sudden wakefulness, annoyed by the intrusion. Flat on his back, eyes wide open, he saw the light bulb in its shade of silver and red, swaying. It looked precarious. Then the powerlessness seized him and held him petrified in its grip.

'Lord God!' he thought.

From the other side of his door, a familiar voice reached out for him, cutting through the fear that surrounded his frantically beating heart.

'Franco, Franco, alzati, get up! C'è un terremoto!

'Earthquake!?'

With trembling legs, he staggered from his bed feeling insignificant in the hand of God.

'Rosaria!' he shouted back. 'We've got to get out!'

The room was rocking and shaking as if the elements outside wanted to get at someone or something inside urgently, yet a quick glance through the window pane showed a serene sky awash with sunshine. He sensed something was not right but could not focus on what it could be. The now had him overwhelmed, chasing his mind far ahead of his reason.

He bumped into a wild-eyed Rosaria in the corridor, wearing a crumpled silk slip and grasping her dress tightly in her hand. They instinctively clasped each other's arms and weaved their way towards the front door. At the same time, the thought rushed into their minds.

'The old man!' they said breathlessly.

Turning towards the living room, they hurried off to get him.

They found him just as they had left him on the sofa the night before except that now his hands gripped the upholstery in a powerful vise and his face, although still asleep, seemed dominant, aggressive and implacable.

Franco felt Rosaria stop and draw back from the forceful and disturbing aura emanating from the old man, but he had a duty to those in his care and pushed through it, reaching out. He shook the supine man, trying to rouse him.

An eye as blue as an open winter's sky when hard frost lies heavily on the stark ground opened and fixed on him. He fell into its vastness and lost all that he was. A sharp pain digging into his neck and shoulder brought him back. He drew in a deep, shuddering breath. Rosaria. She had her hand clawed into his skin, and her face, bloodless and white, was close, peering over his shoulder with terror in her eyes. The room, strangely, no longer shook and they both pulled away, hugging desperately to each other; seeking to hold onto a world that was familiar and safe.

'Merciful All-father!' whispered Franco.

***

The old man spiralled deeper and deeper into a fathomless sleep feeling the swirling mists and shadows of unwanted dream pulling him inexorably closer and closer. He did not want to go there but was unable to control his destiny. He drifted downwards in slow circles, fearful of the knowledge that he might find in the depths but at the same time, curious. His missing eye itched and throbbed with anticipation and uncertainty, unwilling to bear that pain again yet at the same time, elated and excited by what he might learn. The sky burst into flames, casting lurid tongues of orange and yellow, licking and cavorting across the cosmos. From a great height, he fell into a bucking saddle, his heart filled with rage and unbreakable fierceness. 'Rack and ruin! Follow me! We ride to break all that comes against us! Follow me! To live and to die, is all the same. Follow me!' He could hear the thunder of thousands of iron-shod hooves as the shining horde answered his call. They were of the brotherhood of the hall. The best of the best. The time of ale drinking was over. Blood and destiny were singing to them, burgeoning their spirits.

His eye fell on that terrible wolf, red tongue hanging from the corner of a savage mouth, long white fangs glistening with dripping spit, eyes cold and blue as the winter's sky when the frost lies heavy on the hard ground. Like to like, strength against strength. He shivered and steered his unmatched steed towards his fate, outdistancing the rest, opening his eye wide to show the undaunted, wild challenge in his heart; unleashed. The sky started to fall, and the world began to shake.

***

The dark-haired man in front of him with kind, if frightened, eyes, was familiar. He tried to hold onto the fading images from deep inside his head, but the antics of the man and the woman were distracting him. They stared at him with awe and trepidation as if he were the manifestation of the second coming of their nailed God. The son was nailed to a tree, but he was not the first. The All-father had been fastened before him, pierced by his own spear, with his own hand. Was that a borrowed image? Was the pain worth it? The indescribable agony? I sacrificed myself to myself. Hung upside down with blood dripping into my all-seeing eye. Was the secret of the witches worth it? Where is all this vaunted knowledge now? Fading with my dreams, carrying my hard fought for wisdom away like the uncaring tide. Thieves! It takes a thief to outwit a thief, and I have found mine and will not allow him to be stolen. Who were these two gawkers? He should know them though they reeked of the one who had taken his place in this world. Still, their blind faith had been shaken. They had looked into my mind's eye and seen things that they thought could not be. They have glimpsed the dissipating essence of my dream. I can still trace the magic in the runes so all is not as lost as I once feared. I can see my reality reflecting in the broken images swimming in the depths of their haunted eyes; a mirror shattering in a thousand pieces and floating away in the darkness of space. I have them now though they do not yet know it.

* * *

Franco's mouth was dry, his throat parched and raw. Each rasping breath burning further moisture from the soft tissues till he feared he would suffocate. He could feel Rosaria next to him, trembling like a leaf in an autumn breeze. He wasn't alone. She too had seen what he had seen. It was not possible to view such things inside another man's head. Maybe the unexpected terror from the earthquake had caused them to hallucinate. But it stopped! It stopped when he looked into that window to another

67

world!

He took a deep breath and calmed his heightened emotions. Blinking he looked again at the man in front of him. All he could see was an old man with a craggy, seamed face. His long, grey hair and beard, lank with dirt and grease, framing his unsmiling face. Folds of wrinkled skin covered where his right eye should have been, but the left was gazing unwaveringly at them. Yes, it was a cold and unnerving colour but just a human eye all the same, unusual though it may be.

'You are a silly fool, Franco,' he thought to himself. 'A bit of shaking and you fall apart.'

Clearing his throat, he addressed Gandalf in a voice he hoped portrayed balance and calmness.

'There has been an earthquake. More will likely follow, and we may have to leave the building in a hurry.'

Gandalf gave the room a quick glance then focused on them again. His expressionless face clearly conveying the message that he thought they were simpletons.

'Well, we think it was an earthquake,' Rosaria quickly stammered, giving a nervous laugh as her words trailed off.

Franco gave her a glare and muttered.

'Thanks for making that sound even weirder!'

She ignored him and continued.

'Why don't you clean up a bit? The shower is that way.'

'Let me apologise for my friend. She tends to be very outspoken when spooked. By the way, how may we call you?'

Without bothering to answer, the old man got up abruptly and slowly shuffled towards the indicated bathroom.

'Small wonders! He understands! Even though he seems to have misplaced his tongue and his manners,' commented Rosaria.

'And your tongue is far too sharp. As for your manners, well, you always lacked in that department so the two of you should become fast friends... lots in common and all that.'

Up yours, Franco! I've had enough excitement for now. I'm off to get dressed.'

'Rosaria?'

'Yes?'

'What just happened?'

'I don't know,' she replied in a small voice and walked away.

* * *

The lice had gone. He stared at his image in the mirror and ignored the smoky, twisting shadows as they formed and reformed behind him, flitting in and out, sometimes familiar, sometimes not. They were getting stronger since his last dream. He had seen them before in shop and car windows, always following him at a distance, lurking, but now they were becoming bolder, demanding his attention. He ran his fingers through his still wet beard and hair. Yes, they had gone. Suddenly. As if his skin had burned them off, expelled from a place that they had no right to be; interlopers and opportunists. Picking up the small scissors lying by the large, white, porcelain basin with its shiny taps of silver, he began to delicately trim his long beard, snip by snip. It was so good to be clean again. He had almost forgotten the luxury of it. This was not just a memory. It was something that just felt right. Something he had lost on his journey. Why had he thought that? A journey implied a destination, but as far as he knew, he had nowhere to go. Those two petitioners outside were crying out for answers so that they could return equanimity and meaning to the routine of their lives. He had none to give them. They must find their own way and only then would he acknowledge them. Even so, their supplications were helping to return the vigour that had been deserting him. He was slowly clawing his way back to his rightful place.

He cleaned and tidied the washing cubicle until all trace of his presence was removed, then with a small show of regret, he climbed back into his still damp clothing. Moving as quietly and smoothly as a wraith, he flowed out of the temporary haven offered to him as a possible future patron without making any sound whatsoever. Gone as if he never was. 'Just like the lice,' he thought and smiled grimly.

CHAPTER XII

They wanted to tie him down. Lock him in a school. Clamp him to a desk. Tether him to a condescending teacher who uses her so-called knowledge as a weapon to demean him and his origins. Bind his hands and feet, his mind, into their way of thinking and acting. Lash him to the cogs of a system based on patronisation and inequality. Crush his spirit with their concept of right and wrong. Skulking underneath the camouflage of good intentions lay their desire to control everyone and everything. To fashion all in an image that was useful to them. Something to exploit. To enrich themselves through the subtle manipulation of the acceptable. He wasn't quite sure who they were, sneaky bastards, but he would have none of it. He would bend, but he would not break. Once again he had given them the slip. Stupid, narrow-minded bastards! Institutionalism! Wasn't that the big word for it? Bastards! They couldn't pretend to want to wash away the dirt on his hands whilst hiding so many sins in their hearts. He would continue to fight to do the things he wanted to do. To do them how he wanted to do them. If he couldn't resist, then he would run. Better to be free than be a rich slave and even worse, not realising the reality of your existence. Blind idiots!

Head down, hands in pockets and a determination that was growing deeper roots with each stride, Tobar made his way across the noisy, quarrelsome city. He was in the mood to challenge everything, and he would confront anybody and anything that tried to stop him from going home. Home! That sounded odd, but home to him was a person who spoke loudly without having a voice and two weeks of pleasant memories. Home was where an old man had done the impossible and pulled him from a racing river, swollen with rage. A river, driven to rise up in protest against the ill-use done to it by the uncaring hands of the people it succoured. 'You throw your poisons and detritus in me and forget that I am your mother.' He wondered how Flora was getting on. Had she been forced into a shelter for the soulless as well? And Greybeard? Where had the old bugger gotten to this time?

He was so lost in his thoughts that they almost caught him. From the corner of his eye, he saw the dark green SUV swerve across the impatient flow of traffic seemingly oblivious to the outraged blaring and honking of horns. He gave this every minute drama only a peripheral glance for this was the usual mess disguised as driving that occurred in this city day after day. To pay attention to it was the same as deciding to take the straight road to madness. The more noise that they made, the more these civilised people felt safe and alive. To tell the truth, his old camp was a much better place to live than in the streets of this city. Take from them and build a big villa back in the mother country. God helps those who help themselves. Even that dream was now dead, gone the same way as his aunt and uncle languishing in a prison cell somewhere that only Christ knew. He had no one there to send his money to.

The SUV's large front tire bounced aggressively up on the curb in front of him, lancing between a parked limousine, spotless and gleaming, and a madly screaming and gesticulating woman in her smart car who was in the act of aiming to secure that rare and opportune parking space for herself. Two men, clan men, leapt out and ran at him. They were fast, but he was more than their match. With reflexes honed from a lifetime of near escapes, he twisted this way and that, avoiding their grasping hands by a hairsbreadth. In the ensuing confusion of shouting locals and door-men, shocked and gawking tourists, and ear deafening car horns, he led his pursuers a merry dance before giving them the slip in the anxious press of the aimlessly roving crowds.

'That was close!' he whispered to himself, drawing desperately at every breath. 'Second time in one day! Bastards! They don't have a clue.'

He remained in the alley between the city bins and the obnoxious stink oozing from them for a slow count of ten then he headed purposefully into a fancy 'twee' tourist-targeted, garment shop. Before the attendant could think to react, he was already standing by the expensive shirts and sweaters on display. Suddenly, he bent over, clutching his stomach as if he was about to be violently sick, and reaching out at the same time, to support himself on the flimsy rack.

'Vai, vai, out!' shouted the attendant in alarm, grabbing him by his back and shoulders and propelling him back out of the door. He stumbled away still clutching at his midsection and retching horribly. As he turned a sharp corner, he straightened, giggling. In his hands was a grey, designer hoodie.

Slipping it over his head, he strolled away casually.

'Always good to keep a hand in,' he thought. 'It will also keep the bastards from spotting me too easily and come in handy tonight when it gets chilly. Even looks nice.'

He felt particularly pleased with himself as he adroitly weaved his way through the packed side streets.

As twilight began to veil the riverside with its dull greyness yet streaking the sky with a subdued yellow and orange light, Tobar descended the stairs, looking for what he once briefly had. He could see the clear signs that the community of the lost had returned and began to feel inexplicably nervous and anxious. Vague and indistinct figures were moving or lounging about without appearing to have any real purpose other than being there. The state did not want the responsibility of housing these people and preferred to turn a blind eye to their plight once no disasters highlighted their presence. Live and let live it seems. If they stayed quiet and unobtrusive, then they could inhabit the place that nobody else wanted at the moment.

Flora's neat, fabricated house was nowhere to be seen. He searched the dark corners sector by sector with his sharp eyes until he discerned a forlorn, bedraggled figure in her trademark floral dress, sitting dejectedly on a pile of damp cardboard. Life it seemed, had taken away what little happiness Flora and fate had gathered around her. Unsure of what to do next, he stood there staring uncertainly.

'Come, boy, we have work to do,' rumbled the thunder in the mountains.

His heart leapt into his mouth, but he wasn't sure if it was from fright or happiness.

'Greybeard, yu bastard!' he exclaimed in surprise.

The old man had already moved past, and he hustled to catch him up. He was moving deceptively fast, his unhurried strides eating the ground. The boy had to hurry.

As soon as Martha saw them coming through the gloom, she leapt to her feet her eyes coming alight with joy. She spread her arms wide and beamed happiness at them, her thin lips stretched in a smile that occupied half of her face. Tobar couldn't help himself. The moment swept him away in its genuine and delightful warmth. He surrendered himself to Flora's tight hug without self-consciousness or embarrassment.

Greybeard stood there observing them with the expression of a stone mountain, the cold blueness of his eye conveying a note of approval even through the dim light. Then he strode past them and dropped his load of blue plastic sheeting and clean folds of cardboard. Where he had obtained them from was a mystery. It looked as if Tobar was not the only accomplished thief on the block.

They watched him as he got to work and the darkness did not appear to affect his industry in any way. His actions were measured and sure as he reassembled Martha's house. Within twenty minutes, a carbon copy of the original stood there, snug against the far wall of the bridge.

He turned, nodded curtly and disappeared into the darkness, leaving them grinning broadly at each other. Hope had returned with one magical act.

Early the next morning, Tobar was back on the streets. He kept as low a profile as he could, the need for caution overriding his usual cheeky confidence and insolence towards those in authority. Now he was working for the angel in the floral dress not just for the sheer joy of putting a middle finger up at those who scorned him and sticking it to them. Nor was he chasing some elusive dream which belonged more to his people than to him as a person. 'Who needs a bloody villa, anyway!'

By mid-morning he had amassed nearly a thousand Euros, stuffed in his pockets and his newly replaced canvas bag. He dropped by a family owned hardware enterprise which was known by his people to do business on the side, cash only, without any questions asked. He watched the comings and goings for nearly two hours before finally slipping in through the cluttered front door. The last thing he needed was to run into someone familiar. The owner, who did not know him but knew to whom he belonged, did not blink an eye but seemed surprised, although he hid it well when Tobar expressed an interest in a straightforward transaction. 'No, I'm not selling nothing, just buying. Nothing wrong with that, is there! Cash in hand, but don't suppose I'll get a discount for that.'

Of course not. He had paid well over-the-odds for his purchase, but he was pleased with it, nonetheless. Whistling a soft, jaunty tune from the old country, he clutched his paper wrapped package close to his body, literally bouncing with each step. Greybeard had started the ball rolling once again. It was now his turn to play his part.

With the harsh cacophony of echoing sirens forming a constant and annoying background curtain of sound -heralding for all to hear the altering of some unknown person's life- Tobar arrived between the impressive stone-clad pillars supporting the arching bridge that covered a lucky few of the community from the elements and the judgmental gaze of those above. He found Flora gazing emptily at the river, her mind long gone before the current. He squatted next to her and casually handed her his heavy package. She came flying back from wherever her scattered thoughts had taken her and ripped away the paper with childish glee. Inside was a gleaming, new, portable cooker. She giggled happily hugging it to her chest as if it were a treasure. In reality, it was, for now, everything was as it should be. She could return to caring for the lost son she had never had; the surrogate husband who had fallen back into her domestic world. Tobar listened to her crooning contentedly, as she rocked gently back and forth to the soft rhythm she was making. Then she finally looked at him with her ever-present smile. Returning her smile, reached into his bag and produced a brand new floral dress, all be it, a bit crumpled and of a different colour and pattern to the one she had been wearing since he had first laid his eyes on her. She stared at it for a long moment, her eyes glistening, then tentatively took it from his offered hand. With a little cry of joy, she sprang to her feet and dashed off to the shelter of her tiny house. Tobar felt a warmth overcome him. He had, on impulse, snatched it from an outdoor stall on his way back. Right from under the nose of the supposedly hawk-eyed street vendor. He was just too clever and quick, and they were far too dull and slow. He was in a league of his own, and this world was made for him to sample from; to take what he needed and desired. 'Easy pickings,' he thought with satisfaction. 'Like crumbs to a pigeon.'

CHAPTER XIII

She knew that she was dying. She had battled all her life to be what she firmly believed she was on the inside. With great personal hardship and suffering, she had fled her homeland across a cold and hostile sea. Fled from a land where the distorted image of masculinity had burned itself into the culture's fabric. Where the minds of young men, and women, had been altered in a parody of that false claim. In the name of God and Jesus they did despicable evil to those they did not understand or in many cases, those who made them uncomfortable with a truth that was too close to their hidden selves. Here in this city of God, she had hoped to have gained understanding and fair treatment. Here she had expected to be allowed to follow her dream to be treated as normal. To have what every woman could claim as her own. Instead, the people had turned their backs on her; defiled her. The church had refused to see her. The priests bowing their heads in convenient prayer and shuffling past her suffering. And the beatings? They had simply continued. Every night, night after night, when the light of day finally lifted into the sky and found her barely able to walk as she sought out a safe enough corner to try to sleep. She had been raped twice by men who had cursed her for being unclean and unnatural even whilst performing their foul deed under the eyes of Jesus. They will be found on judgement day. Now all she could feel were the broken bones grating together inside her abused body. Huddled under her blankets -gifted by a kind-eyed man who offered her hot coffee and a chance to talk like a human being whenever they had met-she lay bleeding from every orifice through which she had been assaulted. Can a cup of kindness ever be measured? This time they had taken the outrage against her person much too far; beyond the bearable limit. This time she was dying.

As she lay shivering, alone and friendless in a foreign land, awaiting the inevitable with a fragmented half prayer playing on her dry lips, she felt her hand taken into a warm, strong, yet gentle, grip. She experienced the presence of a god. An immortal with compassion as vast as the sky. A guardian who did not come to save. Who was drawn to her because she had fought to the end. He had come to claim her indomitable spirit. To guide her to a place where she would be expected to play her part when the time was right. The reject of one god was the prize of another. She did not feel bitter. She felt rewarded at last as her final breath slipped away from the empty shell that was her body and her spirit was finally allowed to shine in the way it was meant to do from the beginning.

Greybeard heard the last shuddering breath as it escaped the battered body of the boy with the painted face. Something unexplainable had urged him through the otherworldly, lamp-lit night to a gloomy, abandoned platform number 10 where the aimless souls of a Christian purgatory tended to congregate to find their peace through the tip of a pointed needle. He had arrived at the end of the one-sided struggle. A struggle where the only bravery that could be found was in the heart of the loser. A heart that continued to beat with the hot passion of what was right against what was wrong. The fiery passion falling in defeat drew him like a moth to a flame. She, for the spirit was undeniably female, now belonged to him. He watched the translucent, incorporeal mist forming in the air over her head and saw a thing that no other man could see. He inhaled deeply, pulling the damp air into his lungs and guided the spirit into him. It was time for her to go home at last where she would be welcomed with warmth and joy at the long table.

With a hand that seemed to perform a benediction, he closed the glassy, open eyes of the shrunken corpse and rose smoothly to his feet. His work was done here for tonight, but there was always more work to be done. Without this seemingly endless duty, he would never be able to recover himself from the deep hole in which he had fallen. He knew this but could not remember any further. He was confident that he would endure to the end if ever there was an end. Of all his peers and companions his endurance was always the greatest. He reached out to hold on to that stray thought, but it dissipated like smoke from a dying campfire.

During daylight hours this city was one of frantic motion and chaos as people try to achieve their dreams by inadvertently spending their energies fulfilling the ambitions of others. At the darkest hours, it became a different place, a different world. It was at these times that Greybeard felt his connection to what he once was at its highest level. In itself, this was not much. The link remained frustratingly elusive and intangible, but it gave him enough for him to pursue his purpose. It was at this time, mostly, that the most courageous could be found. Stripped of everything, their true essence became more evident, and in their last minutes, he went to them. Those who battled fiercely to the very end, despite the overwhelming odds, were the most significant of prizes to possess.

Somewhere nearby, another soul was trapped in despair, darting this way and that to find a way out. Even so, he felt its challenge, a tremor, a ripple through the thread that binds us all, illuminating the runes that he had bled so much to see. He moved on, following the signs through a man-made twilight world, heading towards the shadow within shadows with a firm and steady step.

At the very door of a basilica on old man sat propped up on the edge of death. He had been here since the sun had risen the day before and could no longer journey onwards. Greybeard knew him. He was once a proud man. A man who would occasionally, on his way to work, drop a coin or two into the plastic cup of a beggar or two to assuage his guilt. Now his cup sat next to him, half-full and unnoticed. He and his brother. They had had a business. They fell out. In his pride and anger, he walked away and plummeted onto the streets into the arms of poverty. His brother grew rich, and filled with regret, tried to find his sibling who he passed every day but did not recognise so changed was he. He had been transformed by the contents of a bottle that soothed and numbed him with its fiery liquid. A medicine to cope with a harsh existence. Lost in shame, he refused to lift his eyes and open his mouth to the man who would be his saviour. And so, as the years marched by, pride kept him bonded to his condition. Then one day, from the shelter of his blanket that covered his head both night and day, he saw the pallor of illness, clawing cancer, sunk deep into the features of his brother as he walked by without seeing what was beneath him. That was the last time, the final chance. Still, he endured in his destitution where his brother could not in his riches. A soul capable of enduring reminded old Greybeard of something fundamental and drew him irresistibly, to the doorstep of a specific basilica in the dead of night. Here he sat in companionable silence, by the side of a man whose liver had been turned to slush, waiting patiently to harvest his enduring soul. 'Your strength to mine and in my strength, I shall make you stronger.'

The dying man somehow knew who Greybeard was, even though he could no longer find the will to open his eyes to look at him. His whistling breath, rasping in and out in the chilled air, reeked of alcohol and the stink of death. Yet, from a place deep inside him, his last thought rattled its way through his opened mouth.

'Brother...'

It was a wish. Greybeard knew what it meant.

In a voice that vibrated protectively around the man, he told the joy and pain of the plain truth.

'There is no place for your brother where you are going. Only those who burn the brightest can find a seat in my hall.'

With understanding and sadness in his heart the man gave up his life, and Greybeard breathed him in.

CHAPTER XIV

'Why did they do it, Franco? She was one of us. You would think they should know better.'

She spoke well. Looking at her you wouldn't have thought it possible. She was fat, dirty and smelt downright horrible but her eyes sparkled with intelligence.

'Being different is sometimes enough, Lisa.'

'Yes, she was different, and that's a God-given fact. We all felt a bit spooked by that, but she was still a human being. No one deserves what they did to her.'

She sipped her coffee and looked angry.

'Do you know who did this to her, Lisa?'

She shook her head.

'Were you the one who found her?'

'No, not me. A station employee on his early shift, I think.'

Franco nodded and sipped his coffee.

The ambulance bolted off, sirens screaming and a group of policemen strutted about looking burly and officious.

'Massimo said that he saw an old bearded man holding her hand and trying to comfort her.'

'What did you say, Lisa? An old bearded man was with her before she died?'

'That's what Massimo said.'

'Do you know where Massimo is now?'

'Gone to hide from our fine guardians here, I suppose. I shall be doing the same before I find myself in prison. Thanks for the coffee, Franco.'

Handing him back his cup, she shuffled quickly away.

'You okay, Franco? You're looking a bit shell-shocked,' observed Rosaria as she hurried over to join him. 'Sadly, nothing here is new. As usual, our good impiegati della municipale haven't got a clue. They are almost implying that she got what she deserved. Callous bastards!'

'Some of them have boots that are not altogether clean, so I'm certainly not surprised,' answered Franco absently. 'Rosaria, I think Gandalf was here with her before she died.'

'What!? Who told you that?'

'Elisabetta. She said that Massimo saw an old greybeard sitting next to her and holding her hand.'

'I see. Do you know how many old greybeards are out there living on the streets, Franco?'

'Yes, yes, you're right. I may be getting carried away, but that man is beginning to disturb me. He isn't normal. I want to talk with

Massimo.'

'Of course you do. We'd better go and find him then.'

'We?'

'Certainly, we. If you're going to play detective, I have no intention of being left behind.'

 They eventually found Massimo sitting in the shade of an Egyptian obelisk. An old haunt of his. Although it was mid-January, the sun was bright and burning. He recognised them immediately but seemed resigned to his fate for he knew what they were after. He had never learnt to keep his mouth shut. Too late now.

 He seemed shy, and even a bit frightened and when they seated themselves on either side of him he visibly shrunk into himself and avoided all eye contact. However, they knew him well, and he was an incorrigible chatterbox.

'Hello Massimo,' greeted Rosaria. 'We know you are a busy man, so we don't want to waste too much of your time. Franco, just wants you to help him in clarifying something that you said earlier.'

 Massimo gave a small, timid smile and said.

'I didn't see anything.'

'Ah,' replied Franco. 'What didn't you see, Massimo?'

'I didn't see that strange, old geezer next to Cyndi.'

'You knew her?' asked Rosaria.

'Sort of. She was real nice. Lent me her magazines and gave me

85

cigarettes now and again. She didn't trust nobody, but she was never afraid. They can't touch my soul, is what she used to say. Only God can have that.'

They sat silently for a few minutes remembering the pure spirit who had met such a terrible and lonely end.

'He goes to some of those who are about to die. She was not the first.'

'What?' asked Franco, unsure of what he had just heard.

'The weird old man. He goes to those who are dying. How he knows, none of us can tell. We are all afraid of him, you see. He seems...indestructible. And very strange. He isn't one of us, for sure. We call him the Soul Stealer.'

'Mary, Mother of God!,' muttered Rosaria.

Franco cleared his throat nervously.

'Does he help them to die, Massimo?'

'Heavens no!' said the little tramp, a bit surprised by the question. 'He just sits there and holds their hands, as far as we can tell. All gentle like. He's freaky, I tell you.'

'Thank you, Massimo. You wouldn't happen to know where he is now, would you?'

'No one but God knows that one and he ain't telling.'

They left the little man as he shifted himself along to remain in the shade, totally unaware that they were no longer there, for he was still chatting away happily.

'We can't believe a word that man says. His mouth runs faster than a fountain.'

'If you say so, Rosaria,' replied Franco in a worried voice.

'What are we going to do?' asked Rosaria.

'We are going to make sure that Cyndi gets a good Christian burial. We owe her that much. We failed her in life. I'm not going to stand by and let the church fail her in death.'

'Amen to that,' muttered Rosaria.

Franco was an advocate sent by the angels and Rosaria was a force despatched from heaven, although some of the priests secretly thought that it surely must have been hell. Their joint effort soon got them noticed and secured a meeting with the local bishop.

'The two of you have a very loud voice. I commend you for your eloquence and persistence. The Holy See has asked that I speak with you and listen to your request. You have captured his attention.'

'Thank you, Your Grace, we...'

'We are tired,' cut in Rosaria. 'A daughter of the church has been refused recognition because of what she felt herself to be in her heart. Didn't Jesus say, 'I have not come to condemn the world but to save it'? Who are we to judge? All we ask is that you open your doors to a sister who loved Jesus and just wanted a fair chance to fulfil a dream to be human like the rest of us. Do we not have the capacity to give her this gift in death even though we failed her in life?'

The room ticked with silent seconds.

'I have personally followed your plea and have wept after reading Cyndi's story. I will support your recommendations. Thank you, my children. You are true servants of God and have reminded us of the simple and powerful message of our Lord Jesus.'

Within two days the church, in the form of three nuns, a priest and the bishop himself, arrived at the city morgue to embrace a cold, unclaimed corpse that the world had had no use for. They took her away and buried her with an intimate and moving ceremony in the bosom of God. Those who mourned for her were many of the homeless, subdued and thoughtful, and charity workers who had tried their best to keep her safe from the vagaries of street life. Politicians and those who wanted to be seen were not invited.

'At least they did something right in the end,' muttered Rosaria.

CHAPTER XV

In the early hours when the community of the lost lay bundled up in whatever was available, the cold dropped on them like a stone from a frozen sky. It seized them and held them firmly in the grip of hoar frost that covered everything in a crusty, icy layer, turning the world brittle, bright and crisp. To those cocooned within the warmth of centrally heated houses, the vista was spectacular. To those outside without choice, it heralded a potential burial shroud. Even the mighty river seemed sluggish in its grasp and flowed along truculently.

The deadening cold pulled Tobar from his sleep. He was coated in white from head to toe, dry frost breaking off like fine powder from his hooded head as he gazed blearily around his frozen surroundings, trying to contain the uncontrollable shivering that wracked his body. He was better off than the rest of the brethren of the river, for his skill allowed him to afford warm clothes and blankets but even so, the frigid air wormed its way underneath his covers in an attempt to leach the living warmth from his thin body. The only person better equipped for this unexpected onslaught from the weather, quiet and deadly, was Flora, who had the added protection of a small hut built around her. Stacking another layer of cardboard beneath him and the icy stone pavement, he covered this with two more layers of blankets and huddled back down to resume his slumber.

It seemed like only minutes had gone by before the thick aroma of coffee reached down into his nostrils and dragged him from his snug blanket cave. Through sleep filled, slitted eyes he saw the cowl wrapped form of Flora tending two coffee percolators on her little stove. He will soon have to fetch her another gas cylinder. A small queue of similarly bound ghosts hovered in front of her patiently, clasping in their hands battered and chipped tin and porcelain cups, all bearing a look of resignation on their ravaged faces. Some carried the swollen features of infection and most certainly alcoholism, the only ointment to soothe a broken and discarded heart from further pain; a panacea for life that hastens the advent of death.

With a stoic effort, he crawled out from under his blankets and folded them into a neat pile, bar one, the thickest, which he swaddled around his head and shoulders. Without making a fuss or staking territory, he joined the file of ghosts and patiently awaited his cup of hot stimulant. Ever smiling, Flora reserved her best smile for him when his turn came and handed him his special cup which she always kept by her side and which he always returned to her after drinking. It was their morning ritual and not even this bone-numbing cold would interrupt it.

Twice that morning, the polizia sauntered down to the community to advise them to seek out the centres newly opened to assist with this freezing snap of inclement weather. Here they would be able to ride out the cold spell and receive hot food and drink. It's going to get worse, they said. Don't be stubborn and foolhardy, they said. Listen and take heed before it's too late. The close-knit community smiled and nodded, but no one bothered to take their advice. The muscular guardians sauntered away, pleased with themselves for performing their civic duty but holding very little expectation that any attention would be given to it. Maybe a bit of bad weather would enable some well-needed culling. They would clean up the unfortunate mess after. Black humour, as always, had its place and served its purpose. Despite this, the community persevered as they always did, through thick and thin.

Not all did, however. After three days and nights of freezing, sub-zero conditions an old man, dark of skin and noble in disposition, cast adrift from a sun-washed, beautiful continent overbrimming with the ills of fate where he once eked out a living as a University professor, succumbed. At night he tended to sit alone, staring into the river, coughing a cough deep and wet inside his chest, sipping from a bottle of forgetfulness and shedding tears of loneliness into the dark waters. Early one morning as everyone else stirred, he remained frozen beneath his covers. The sadness of their reality was so stark that none of the community had room for tears although they felt the loss deeply. Instead, they had to hearken to the 'I told you so,' time and time again from the frowning and disapproving polizia. 'For your own good, you should listen to us.' Once again they nodded in agreement and continued with the task of living. 'Let the dead bury the dead.'

When the little community was at their lowest ebb, they were invaded by the worse that the homeless had to offer. Within this element were mostly young men, a few with female companions met on the road of shared misfortune and enforced circumstances. They were known and mentioned rarely without an accompanying shudder, as the 'Punkabbestia'. These 'Gutter Punks' were like jackals, strutting boisterously and aggressively along the river bank and on the bridges spawning above, making a noisy nuisance of themselves among the rest of the homeless who just wanted to be invisible and left alone. However, these restless chasers of the devil's tail, snared by drink, drugs and a river's weed, roamed the breadth of their domain with disruptive and sometimes deadly mischief. Desensitised to cold and discomfort through the use of readily available chemical substances, their memories suspended by a hallucinogenic fog, they were not always aware of the hurt they caused to the fallen with whom they shared their world. Be that as it may, this did not make their actions and the resulting consequences tolerable or excusable.

Out of the hazy cold that dampened the river and its surroundings, they descended on the small community like a pack of disorganised, wild dogs, barking and snapping, in jovial disharmony. The frightened denizens, shy of any confrontation whatsoever, grabbed the most precious of their possessions and melted away. Those few who remained huddled in on themselves, and without any protection but their vulnerable minds, tried to find refuge in that inner world of unclear thoughts. The jackals, laughing and playing, pulled and scattered the paltry remnants of the belongings left behind by those who had fled, seeking out what they could scavenge. Not all ran or hid.

Refusing to be intimidated, Martha sat by her priceless cooker, her eyes focused with an inner determination at the river as it flowed by. The jackals fanned out and padded towards the small figure swathed in her blanket, unmoving.

'Nice cooker you have there, signora. It's just the thing we need,' said their leader, a slender, hard-muscled man of about thirty years with long, blond dreadlocks and a scraggly beard.

His companions giggled insanely like hyenas at his nasty, uncaring words.

Still, Martha did not move or acknowledge their presence.

'Did you hear me, signora?' asked dread-locks.

'A' Ste, she is as mad as the rest of them. Just take the bloody thing,' encouraged a haggard, blank-eyed girl of about eighteen years who, despite the biting cold, was wearing a pair of dirty shorts. 'I fancy a nice brew tonight. You know how I like it hot.'

More mad sniggering echoed around her announcement.

'I'm sorry, signora, but that's mine now,' said the pack leader, stretching out his arm to take what was not his.

With waspish speed, Martha flew at him, snatching her prized possession clean from his surprised hands and crouching low and protectively over it, hissed at him like an outraged cat defending its territory. He was momentarily taken aback by her aggressive response but then flushed anger suffused his hard-boned features, and he stepped forward, raising his sinewy hand with violent intent.

From his icy corner, enwrapped from head to toe in his frost encrusted blankets, Tobar watched the scene unfold. He was no stranger to conflict and bullying confrontation. He had been born into it and reared up with it. It was as normal to him as a cereal breakfast is to a middle-classed, English schoolboy. Unnoticed or ignored, he followed Flora's fiery defence of what was hers with sharp, keen eyes. He tracked the arm of outraged retribution being raised to slap her down into cowering submissiveness. In one fluid motion, he moved from his folded position with the reflexes of one who had always lived on the edge and who was born with a little more to draw on than most. Exploding out of his blankets in a puff of dislodged frost, he launched himself at the bully aggressing his Flora without thought of consequence or strategy. Life is there to be met head-on; ask nothing, give everything. He closed the gap with incredible speed, and as that spiteful hand descended towards its defiant target, it was intercepted by a glint of steel in a ray of frigid sunlight.

'Fuck! Fuck! The little bastard cut me!' screeched the would be punisher. 'Don't just stand there! Get the little fucker!'

Nasty words, from a nasty man.

Tobar stood in front of a still hissing Flora, his pocket knife weaving a slow figure eight. Compared to the five-membered band of Gutter Punks he was small but his expressionless face communicated complete and deadly commitment. Outnumbered and outsized they still hesitated. They had not expected this.

'Get him! Get him,' screamed the bleeding dreadlocks, clasping his hand tightly in an attempt to stem the red flow and looking around furiously for a weapon.

Just as his eyes landed on a loose, broken grey brick and bent to pick it up, one of his pack slithered over to him and whispered nervously.

'We'd better go, mate. It's him again.'

Eyes flashing with fury and confusion, dreadlocks cast his gaze this way and that trying to discern what the hell his pack mate was talking about. The others were already drawing away, their shifty eyes focused on something coming towards them that made them uncertain and afraid.

Striding unhurriedly along the walkway towards them was a tall man with a long grey beard and hair. On his head was a felt hat pulled low over his face and a long, waxed, dark brown coat which hung from his broad shoulders. He exuded an air of grim implacability like a mountain sliding slowly towards the sea. He gave the impression of great age yet immense strength all at the same time. As he strode through the now freezing fog that had floated across the smoking river, the air, mist mixed with sunlight, seemed to ebb and flow, dissipate and coalesce, in an ever-shifting halo around his silver grey hair. Tobar felt the small hairs at the back of his neck rise up, and a shiver ran through his body as if the icy particles in the air were being energised by an unknown source.

'Cazzo!' muttered the pack leader, finally seeing what was spooking his band of misfits. 'Shit! Shit! Let's go.'

 They hurried off the way they had come, craning their necks around to track the progress of the object of their fear. What had caused them to react in such a manner? The drug-crazed 'Punkabbestia' were unpredictable and nasty, but their chosen coping mechanisms had left them devoid of all ordinary human feelings, fear included. What then could have happened between them and old Greybeard to have awakened an emotion that should have long been silenced inside their chemically altered brains? Tobar was intrigued.

'Hey, Greybeard,' he shouted. 'Where yu been, mate? Yu old bastard! What you done to them shit-heads anyway? Told their stinky secrets to their mothers or something? They scared of you, mate. Maybe it's that hexing eye of yours, eh? Scares the shit out of me too.'

In spite of his cheeky levity, Tobar was a bit perturbed. There was something about Greybeard that was very different. Yes, he still looked old, but now he seemed powerful and indestructible. 'Been at the energy drinks, I suppose,' he thought, trying internal humour to release some of his unease. It didn't work.

The old man stopped in front of them and fixed them with his eye. Tobar averted his gaze before he fell into the sky. The man looked the same, but there was a feeling about him that was different as if he had become a giant. Flora though did not seem overawed in the least. She grinned up at the unsmiling Greybeard and patted him on his chest which to Tobar's disconcertion, also appeared to have attained a greater breadth.

Surprising them all, Greybeard did not do his usual disappearing trick but settled down next to them on the cold stone as if he were on a sandy beach in the Bahamas. Ever the one to take full advantage of a situation, the young lad seized on the presented opportunity to learn more about the enigmatic Greybeard.

'Never did thank you for pulling my carcass out of the river,' he began, nodding his head at the rushing water which was running just a foot below the lip of the walkway. A little more rain and we will have to scarper again, he thought.

'Fingers crossed, eh!' he muttered.

He had not expected a response from Greybeard, and in fact, he did not get one.

'Why do you help me out, Greybeard? In my experience, people only give when they want something in return.'

'I need you to steal something that was once mine.'

The voice rumbled over him like rocks grating on boulders in an immense and ponderous glacier.

'Why didn't you just say so? Point the way, and I'll fetch it for you.'

'Not even you can reach it where it lies. When the time is right, I will take you there.'

'Just let me know boss man. I'm ready anytime.'

'It is you who will determine the hour. I will guide you from that point. Your reward will be great.'

'I don't need no payment. I owe you my life twice over.'

Greybeard was so silent that Tobar wasn't sure if he had heard.

'What you want me to steal anyway?'

The silence stretched out once more. Then when the answer finally came, he wasn't sure if he had heard right for it made no sense.

'My memory. You must bring it back to me.'

Tobar concluded that Greybeard was one of them mad schizophrenics after all. The poor bugger had lost his mind. His memory was the least of his problems, poor old bugger.

Even so, the next few days after were pure bliss for him. He felt he finally had a family worth having, imperfect as it was. There was Flora, fussing over him and trying to meet his every need in her own peculiar way. Then there was Greybeard. Not exactly a father figure. More like a mysterious and eccentric grandfather

97

who had half his mind in a world that no one else could see. Happiness, he decided, was a strange, unmeasurable and unpredictable thing.

CHAPTER XVI

'The polizia have been sticking to my shoe like old gum for the past few weeks. Can't seem to be able to scrape them off. They've even mentioned your names a couple of times.'

 Franco and Rosaria gazed innocently at their supervisor and longtime associate. He returned their look keenly then with a sigh continued.

'They seem to somehow think that you might be able to help them with their enquiries but both of you are refusing their calls. They are especially looking for a young, Romani boy, aged between 12 and 14. A one-man crime wave apparently and very slippery. Covered with grease they say. Impossible to get a grip on and as far as being streetwise, well, he is in a class of his own. I reminded them that our charity is not in the business of helping the police track down those fallen into misfortune on our streets but to render them aid as the Lord teaches us. Still, they insisted that they would highly appreciate it if you would consent to just speak with them bearing in mind past favours and all that. I'm not quite sure what that meant and neither I think, do I want to know. May Jesus be your conscience.'

 He paused once again to eye them over the rim of his thick, dark glasses. They still sat there, silent, demure and saintly. Making a small grunting noise, he ploughed onwards.

'Another person of interest to them is an old man with long grey hair and beard. Apparently, he has the habit of being in close proximity to those who the Lord has called to his bosom. They would very much like to interview him and think it very likely that you have knowledge of his whereabouts. If this man is engaging in some kind of self-styled euthanasia, maybe it is wise to help our law enforcement colleagues out a bit. We can't have anyone playing god on the streets now, can we?'

'Are you aware of how that request sounds, Stefano?,' said Rosaria. 'Are you even listening to yourself? An old man with long grey hair and beard playing god! Sounds like a prank a juvenile would make on the man controlling the tannoy at an airport. If you find a man of this description, please take him to the nearest chapel.'

'Alright, alright. I get your point. Still, if there is any substance to this at all, please reconsider.'

'Okay, Stefano,' replied Franco. 'Are we done for now? I'm dying for a coffee.'

'You've become addicted to that stuff, Franco. Beware vices.'

'Thanks for the advice, Father Stefano.'

As they hurried out of the building, Rosaria commented sharply.

'That Massimo has been running his mouth again it seems. The man can't help himself!'

'It's his only pleasure in life,' replied Franco. 'Besides, I still can't track down Gandalf although with this cold snap I've hardly had the time to look for him. Any word on your end?'

'Not a smidgen, but there is some connection between him and that boy by the river. That may be a good place to start.'

'Martha?'

'Martha.'

'Good idea, Rosaria. Shall we?'

'Why not.'

The weather had miraculously transformed itself, becoming warm and balmy, the sun shining down with bright, uninterrupted enthusiasm as if the icy coldness of a few hours past belonged purely to the realm of the imagination.

After spending a frustrating fifteen minutes looking for a space to park her car, Rosaria slotted it into a spot not entirely legal and trusted in the goodwill of Jesus. Then trotting behind a long-striding Franco, they weaved their way through the packed throng of tourists and their predators, the ever hopeful street hawkers and opportunists.

'God, what a mess!' muttered Rosaria.

Franco had to agree with her but did not let on. He didn't really want to encourage her into her usual waspish and well-repeated observations on city life. Her family was originally from a small village in the mountains, and deep inside her, this village still lived on. There was a saying that described her situation perfectly, but he was too preoccupied to think of what it was.

They entered under the sheltering umbrella of the line of trees, sentinels atop a defensive wall between a force of nature and a man-made refuge, demarking one zone from the next, forming a dim leafy curtain between two worlds. Then, almost unexpectedly, they came upon the easily overlooked stairway that led down to the river's embankments.

They passed a few members of the community lying in the sun, soaking up the warmth directly and through the stones. Some were reading books and magazines, and some were just stretched out indulging in empty thoughts. Martha was the only one sitting under the shade of the bridge, and she was alone.

'Ciao, Martha. Got your house back, I see,' greeted Franco. 'It looks fantastic! You must give me the name of your builder. He has a good eye.'

Martha looked at them and smiled. A smile that was both weary and wary. Franco was taken aback. He had never seen that look from her before. Her smile had always been open. Now she had something, no, someone to protect.

'To be honest, Martha, we were hoping to talk with your young friend. Only to talk, mind you, we will not be the ones to take him from you. We think he might be able to give us a clue as to where to find Gandalf.'

Martha's smile remained the same, but her eyes shifted for a split second. She knew something, but she no longer trusted Franco with this knowledge. A deep sadness fell over Franco. Instinctively, he reached out and touched Martha's shoulder.

'Tell them that the polizia is looking for them and if they get caught to send for either myself or Rosaria. We will come to stand by their sides.'

Martha blinked and looked away. Yes, they were both there with her, either visiting frequently or even sleeping near her.

'Thanks, Martha. Don't let anything or anyone take away your smile. You know and where to find me if you have a need.'

'What was that all about!' whispered Rosaria fiercely as they walked away. 'We were supposed to ask questions not act as an early warning system for possible fugitives.'

'Martha has already answered our questions.'

'What?'

'Both Gandalf and the boy are staying down here with her.'

'How do you know that!? Ah, yes, stupid me. I should open my eyes more and my mouth less.'

'Yes, you should.'

'Watch it, mister! It's the house, isn't it? An exact copy of the first which Gandalf built. And of course, the cooker. Martha does not have the money or the means to acquire such quality.'

'Only a master thief could provide such a gift.'

'Why didn't we just wait until they return?'

'You know the answer to that. In our work, God's work, trust is everything. We will drop back in at a later date. Give them the time and space that they need.'

'Sometimes you're so sanctimonious, Franco.'

He smiled.

CHAPTER XVII

Days slipped by into weeks, and although the movements of the community took on a rhythm of their own, the comings and goings of Tobar and Greybeard remained undisturbed and undetected by the occasional checks made by the police and by the concerned noses of the social services. This was more by fate than by design. They even managed to be absent when Franco and Rosaria dropped by with a community volunteer doctor in tow. The doctor gave all who were present as thorough a medical as was possible under the circumstances and handed out a few antibiotics. She seemed particularly concerned about Martha whose health had always been delicate and encouraged her to visit the nearest hospital for a more in-depth examination. They all watched her smile and knew that she would not. The community, on the whole, appeared to be well supplied. They had blankets, sleeping bags and even a few tents. Most of them wore suspiciously new coats and shoes. Franco almost expected to see tags still hanging from them. The influence of the Romani boy's skills was everywhere. The polizia, God bless them, would not have failed to notice this. It would not take long for them to lay down their snares.

Tobar watched all this unfolding from high up on the river wall, leaning precariously over the chipped edge and observing everything with his sharp eyes which rarely missed anything. Sad as it was, his days here were numbered. If he was playing it wisely, he should have already been long gone, but he couldn't bring himself to leave yet despite noticing the iron jaws of city justice getting ready to snap shut. He realised that Greybeard felt the same for his movements were once again elusive and unpredictable. He seemed to be continually on the move, never staying in one place for long. Never getting tired, never getting cold, never showing any signs of distress or discomfort. How did the old bastard do it? The only thing that appeared to give him pause was the simple act of going to sleep, although this too he only seemed to need a little of. Whenever he did succumb, he appeared to be immediately ensnared by violent dreams which made him toss and turn and which, frighteningly, seemed to affect the dreams of anyone else lying around in his vicinity. Most times he would wake up abruptly and walk away without an explanation or farewell, no matter the hour of the night. He would never get accustomed to the strangeness of the man. As for those two do-gooders and Jesus botherers. They were making a right nuisance of themselves. They had the knack of popping up all over the place. He refused to give the time of day to anybody who hid behind all that religious malarkey. However, there was no doubting the fact that Flora liked them, especially the dark-haired bloke, and that Greybeard was familiar if not altogether comfortable with their presence. That had to count for something. Some would say that he had been spending an awful amount of time sneaking about and poking his nose into other people's business, but he didn't see it that way. To survive and to be one step ahead of the competition, one had to be informed. There were too many geezers out there who were hoping that you were misinformed so that they could get one over on you. With your enemies, which was just about everyone he could think of except Flora and Greybeard, he knew where they were at and kept an eye out for them. Flora and Greybeard were family. He trusted them. That is why he had to go out of his way to make sure that this trust wasn't misplaced. Hence the sneaking and snooping. Like it or not, a man's got to do what a man's got to do, and a man's got to look out for himself on the street. Number one first then the rest.

What Greybeard had said was still worming its way around in his head. Was the man serious? At first, he had dismissed his words as just the echoes of a lunatic. Yes, Greybeard was mad alright, but then again the old bugger was surrounded by opaque oddness, oddness that shouldn't be possible. He had looked at these things from every angle. He knew how to do that. His livelihood depended on it. He still couldn't find the right way in. Steal back his memory! He had to ask himself again. Was the man serious? He had a sinking feeling that maybe he was. Where would that leave him? Not in a good place for bloody sure. He had had a friendly chat with that locomotive mouth sitting like a scarecrow in the shadow of Cleopatra's needle. He hadn't liked what he had heard one bit.

It had been nothing else but the interfering hand of fate. He had been out making money when he had spotted the two prayer whisperers making a beeline for the centre of the piazza. Being an over-curious bugger, he had followed them to see what was holding their attention so fast. Low and behold, he saw them capture Mr Motor-mouth in a pincer movement of clinical execution. After that, he just had to know. Bloody well now wish he hadn't. 'Soul-stealer! Santa Madonna!' Far worse than being accused of child stealing.

As the two knee-benders and the far too elegant for the street doctor emerged out of the cracked after-thought that served as the entrance to the stairs that connected existence below with

the normality of life above, Tobar trailed after them at a discreet
distance. Adaptability to any presented situation was his
trademark and one of the keys to his success. He noted their
many and varied stops and mapped their network. He needed to
know how dangerous they might be or alternatively, how useful.
He needed to see who they knew and how the route back from
these points might threaten the position of his whereabouts and
activities. He needed to know how much more they knew about
Greybeard. He needed to know if they were two-faced stooges of
authority, happily looking in both directions at the same time or
members of that endangered species of genuine souls.
Information, no matter how useless, was always useful.

After about three hours of a slow, stop and start progress, the
doctor waved farewell to her good Samaritan guides and went her
own way. The two then set off more briskly. At least they walked
and didn't cruise around the city in style dishing out their sacred
works to those who could never acquire what they had. He had to
give that to them; they sweated and got foot blisters for their
cause. Good on them.

An endless stream of visitations on homeless buggers followed
one after the next. Finally, as the pair stopped to talk to a big-
bellied, black-bearded man who looked more like a wrestler than
a vagrant, Tobar felt the wind suddenly dessert his sails. The
trade-mark coffee came out, and the slow, casual chat began.
Tobar had had enough. What was he doing anyway? He was trying
to put meaning into an empty situation. He didn't belong to the
cosy little community where Flora hid from a life she could not
forget. He couldn't be tied down to such an existence. It was
useless for him to attempt to hold on to something he had never
had. If he deluded himself any longer, he would soon find himself

staring at Miss Tight-pants' seams again. He didn't want that, and he was sure neither did she. Leaning against the side of a fountain he made his decision. He would buy Flora something really lovely and leave his full bag of money with her. Whether that was a good idea or not, that was what he was going to do. As for Greybeard, well, he was tired of mysteries. It was time to move on.

Almost in resignation, he pushed himself away from the noisy and irritable muttering of tumbling water and turned to retrace his steps. As he did so, he saw the unmistakable SUV bearing down on him from ahead. As usual, he instinctively did the unexpected. Instead of racing off along the pavement in the opposite direction, he darted directly across the street in front of the oncoming vehicle causing it to swerve dangerously in a squealing of brakes and gripping tyres. This immediately drew everyone's eyes to its no-good activities. Unfortunately, two pairs of those drawn eyes belonged to members of the Carabinieri who were sitting in their parked car unnoticed at the side of the busy thoroughfare. As if it were a bad movie, Tobar's gaze locked onto theirs at the same time as theirs's locked on to his. Twisting like a dancer, he dived back into the moving traffic and failed to see a driver in his white van aggressively and wildly switching lanes for no other better reason than to get ahead of the next car. The boy's reactions were superb. He leapt into the air like an acrobat knowing that he didn't have the time or space to avoid the oncoming rushing vehicle. He landed with both feet on the bonnet with the surprised driver blaring his horn in panic, a look of terror on his face. Despite his agility, the forward momentum of the van was far too rapid, and he was catapulted over the windscreen and roof of the impatient machine. Like a cat he landed on his feet but lost his balance and fell heavily onto the rough, uneven asphalt, skidding along its unforgiving surface. For Tobar, everything seemed to be happening both too fast and too slow all at the same time. He dragged himself to his feet feeling a lancing pain in one of his ankles and his knee. He glimpsed the shredded sleeve of his designer wear hoody and felt the blood trickling down underneath it as cars jammed on their brakes in a mad display all around him. The twisted hands of fate were not through with him yet. One car, driven by a young, man who had been busily engaged in a narcissistic moment with his mirror, did not see him in time to terminate his speed and in his startlement, depressed the wrong peddle. Instead of stopping, his small, newly bought car, spurted forward, slamming into the dazed Tobar and sending him flying into the back of another vehicle. His head struck the quick shatter, webbed glass with gut-wrenching force, sending the bloodied Romani boy sliding barely conscious to the street. Tobar, to the shocked eyes of all witnesses, pulled himself to his feet once again. He was hardly aware and had no idea of what had just happened but with a will of pure steel and a survival instinct unmatched he hobbled away quickly, noting on a subconscious level the concerned look of the two Carabinieri officers as they tried to get through the blocked traffic to render him assistance. 'For fuck's sake!' he thought. 'All that and the muskers hadn't even recognised me!'

 Across the street, Franco and Rosaria had turned at the commotion. They were rooted in horror as they watched the boy spiral through the air. Then in amazement, as he crawled to his feet followed quickly by sheer dread as he was hit by yet another car. They continued to stare helplessly as the boy, incredibly, pushed his battered and bleeding form onto his feet and limped away through the petrified drivers and onlookers. In the blink of an eye, he had disappeared from view.

'Jesus, oh Jesus!' exclaimed a shaking Rosaria, her voice brimming with sorrow and emotion. 'Wasn't that our boy!? Oh, Jesus Franco! We've got to help him!'

'He's long gone, Rosaria. We'll never find him now, but I have a fair idea where he'll go. Come, let's catch a taxi.'

CHAPTER XVIII

Greybeard was sitting in a deserted and overgrown private garden under the shadow of an ancient ruin, stones stained and moss covered. He wasn't quite sure how he had gotten there but didn't really care. The combination of time linked stone edifices constructed by pagans from a long dead era and the nearness of the branches of the One Tree that bonded the world together gave him the illusion of having a peaceful mind. He was grateful for this. He had to leave this city. He had overstayed his welcome. The Jesus God was closing in. Still, he had to wait on the boy. His skill was needed. The renewed strength teasing his limbs was not enough. The return of the black raven was essential and long overdue. Hidden in the boy was the spirit of the wolf; a companion from the beginning of the ages. Only the wolf had the skill to find memory and guide him through the many dangers back into his mind. 'All that is me must return to me.' He turned the strange words around in his head and tried to examine them objectively. As usual, they slipped away like smoke caught in a draft. Then he heard something urgent echoing faintly along the roots and vines of the One Tree. One pulsing vibration among a myriad of others but it held a message meant only for him, illuminating the runes that he had shed his blood to understand. The sisters of destiny were playing their age-old games, but they were no longer the only masters. Knowledge was everything, and the pursuit of it was all abiding.

Abruptly, he rose to his feet in one fluid motion and set off, each resolute foot-fall rekindling the smouldering magic deep within the earth, guiding him onwards. Such a blatant display of his power would surely hasten the Christ to him but he was close to his goal and the risk was worth the harvest waiting to be reaped.

***

Tobar was swimming in a sea of pain. He gritted his cracked teeth and smothered the sobs that threatened to tear themselves from his blood filled mouth. Bones were broken, and something terrible had happened to him inside. He had known pain before but never like this. His sight wavered, and his world shrank in tight around his agony. Sweat and blood constantly dripped into his eyes, and he kept wiping it away, smearing his face garishly, each time he made one of his frequent stops to rest and gather himself. The good citizens made wide circles to avoid him when they saw him dragging along, staring at him in horror or averting their eyes, pretending that they had not seen him. He did not care at all. He did not want their help or their pity. 'I won't give in, you bastards! I won't give in.' His body was shaking from head to foot, and one of his legs was almost useless; no feeling whatsoever, in it. He dragged it behind him as an actor would parody a lame man but this was no pretence. He had to get to Flora. 'Mother of God!' He had one last gift for her. Clasping his bag to his broken ribs in the grip of death he fixed her image firmly in his mind and crawled his way home, inch by groaning inch.

***

For most of her waking hours, Flora's mind lay on an endless empty plain where the sun coloured the grey sky in a perpetual attempt to rise up in it. She was usually content with this, but today something was different. It was as if swarms of insects had been stirred up and were now intent on biting and stinging her to distraction in her place of solitude, demanding her attention with their pestilence. She did not know why this was happening but interpreted it as a sign that something had gone terribly wrong. For her the only thing going right in her life was Tobar. The resulting conclusion left her fretful and anxious. It was impossible for her to sit at her cooker dolling out hot coffee to the community. Instead, she erratically patrolled the confines of the space under the bridge like a demented bird, spreading her anxiety like an infectious virus to the others, driving them to seek sanctuary, heads covered to shut the world out, under their sleeping bags and blankets.

The sudden and frenetic appearance of Franco and his companion did not improve her state of mind. Standing there uncertainly, wings spread ready to take flight, she watched them nervously as they hurriedly descended the stairs and ran over to her.

'Martha, have you seen your friend? The Romani boy? Has he returned?'

Franco's words tumbled out. A disturbing anomaly, as he was always so calm, measured and friendly. He was renowned for portraying an image of lucid reasoning, giving out an impression that everything could be solved, so there was never a need to worry. Now, he had turned this long time assurance on its head.

Fixing her agitated eyes, filled with pleading, on Franco's face, Martha shook her head vigorously and frantically. The stream of questions, banned from a forgotten tongue, pouring from dilated pupils in a gush of panicked concern.

'There's been an accident. We think he has been badly hurt. We thought he might come here. We have to find him.'

Tears sprung like a burst well from Martha's eyes, and she shook like a leaf in a storm.

Immediately, Rosaria enfolded her in a comforting embrace, holding her fragile and shaking body close, stroking her unwashed hair.

'Stay with her,' said Franco. 'I'll go...'

Before he could finish his sentence, a figure came into view at the top of the stairway. It swayed and stumbled as if drunk, missing the first step and in a desperate grabbing motion, clung onto the stone handrail as a sailor would cling to a broken mast in high seas. Even from this distance, it was clear that it was the boy in question and that his face was as white as a newly laundered sheet, devoid of all colour, like that of a death's mask.

'Jesus, Mary and Joseph!' prayed Rosaria. 'Franco...'

The man was already racing towards the stairs, his heart beating as fast as his flying feet. Martha collapsed into Rosaria's arms, her eyes rolling up into her head, eyelids fluttering irregularly, and saliva drooling down from the corner of her mouth. She appeared to be having a small epileptic seizure. Rosaria eased herself down onto the cold stone taking the little woman with her and supporting her on her lap. Behind her, the denizens of the community rose up like grey ghosts in a graveyard, hesitant and shy in coming forward.

Bolting up the stairs two at a time, Franco could see that the boy was in bad shape. He was barely conscious, and it was obvious that he was now utterly incapable of supporting his own weight. His head and face were covered in dry blood, and his features were swollen and disfigured. He was mumbling something softly over and over again, and his eyes were the mirrors of infinite pain.

'I've got you now, old fellow. You can let go now. I'll take you down to Martha. She is waiting for you with a warm cup of coffee,' said Franco gently.

'Don't need no help,' replied the boy faintly, then passed out.

Franco lifted him into his arms, surprised of how light he was, and carried him carefully down to the walkway. As he got to where Rosaria sat cuddling the diminutive form of Martha, one of the grey ghosts drifted over with a pile of blankets and laid them out on the cold flooring. Franco slowly lowered the boy on one then helped Rosaria place Martha on the other.

'Seeing him like that was too much for her, I think. Hope she didn't get a stroke. Poor girl. He looks in bad shape, Franco. We ought to call an ambulance. For both of them.'

Franco knew that she was right yet still he hesitated. Urgent medical attention was what they certainly needed, but on the other hand, he felt that he would be engaging in a gross act of betrayal. With a deep sigh, he reached for his mobile. A shadow fell on him.

'Gandalf!?'

He seemed bigger, broader, taller. Immense and vast. A mountain with its top shrouded in the clouds. Grim and brooding.

'When...How did...?'

It was not just to do with physical size. He exuded power, force, an implacable will and purpose. A giant.

Franco looked into his eye and fell onto the open field of a glacier forming a bridge under a clear blue sky. He was swallowed and lost. A mere speck as the worlds spun on forever in space and time.

With a supreme effort, he shook himself free of the vision only to find that the old man had already walked past and was kneeling next to the fallen boy, holding his hand softly in his.

A mixed look of fear and horror was etched into Rosaria's features as the chilling words of Massimo scribbled themselves across her mind. 'We call him the Soul-stealer.'

Franco quickly hurried over to join them.

'He has been badly injured in a car accident. We have to call an ambulance.'

'Greybeard? What took you so long?'

The weak voice interrupted Franco and drove him to silence, his phone gripped forgotten in his hand.

'A pretty lady with a bright face. Do you see her? She is sitting on a white horse and keeps calling my name.'

Martha suddenly opened her eyes and sat up, holding Tobar's other hand in hers. He smiled at her.

'This is for you Flora,' he whispered, pulling his hand away and nudging his canvas bag towards her. 'Wanted to buy you something nice but...bastards.'

He turned his tired eyes which were losing their brightness back to Gandalf.

'Greybeard? I told her that I was waiting for you. That I had promised to help you out. Too late now...sorry.'

Then a low thunder rolled over them, making Rosaria and Franco jump with the unexpectedness of it.

'The Valkyrja are mine. They do my bidding. Our bargain is still binding. I will take you personally across the bridge. They shall be our escort.'

Both Franco and Rosaria stared at Greybeard with their mouths hanging open; dumbstruck.

Greybeard rose to his feet smoothly and effortlessly, bearing the dying boy in his arms. He turned and strode solemnly along the stone walkway towards the waiting river, not sparing a glance for either of them.

'Stop, Gandalf!'

Rosaria had found her voice.

'You can't do this! The boy needs urgent medical attention!'

Greybeard stopped, but it wasn't for her. His sky filled eye fell on Martha.

'We will wait for you,' he said quietly and turned once again to continue on his dread path.

'Gandalf! Where are you going? What are you doing?' shouted Franco, raw despair in his voice.

He desperately needed to stop this madman but could not think of how to do it. He desperately needed to stop this insane scene from playing out, but could not think of how to do so. His feet and will had been turned to clay. His mind numb and forlorn.

Head held high as he gazed at something that no one else could see the man who had lost his mind walked on his inevitable path to the churning river. Just as his leg lifted to step off of the edge, a fog swirled in off the green water and he and the boy in his arms were lost to sight.

Behind him, Franco heard a distressed wail of hopelessness from Rosaria that sent a chilling finger of realisation racing up his spine. What had he just witnessed!? He ran to the river but could find no sign of the offering that surely must have fallen into its depths. With trembling fingers he punched the button that would connect him to the emergency services, blinking the hot tears from his eyes.

'Too late, Franco. You're much too late!'

The thought echoed over and over in his suspended mind.

Hours later as they huddled in blankets, shocked and listless as the divers searched and dragged the river's bottom tirelessly, Franco's phone gave out its jaunty little tune.

'Pronto?' he answered automatically. It was the doctor from the hospital.

'Franco, I'm sorry, but the little lady in the floral dress that you sent to us has just passed away. We think that her heart just gave out. She had a bag full of money with her. Do you know anything about it?'

Franco let the phone drop from his hands. He did not have the strength to answer. Maybe tomorrow.

EPILOGUE

'Wayfarer, Wanderer, beggar, king and god. I am all these things and more.'

The old gods are still with us, some believe. Kept alive by those who are fascinated with a lost world which the theological curtain of Christianity has separated from us. A name spoken, written, thoughts and theories, all agitate the dormant runes. With each weakened pulse, travelling through the roots of the world, a stiffened limb is animated, a neuron in a mind, vast and old, sparks. A god who was never quite a god, becomes aware of thought and memory. Another crack in the stasis that binds him. Stronger than all, wiser than all, built to endure, he remembers who he once was. He is a survivor. He knows what is needed to continue seeking. What was known and what still lies out there to be discovered. He is driven and needs the best of the best to believe once again. With their strength, he becomes stronger and in turn, lends them strength. In an alien world that no longer belongs to his kind, he struggles. He battles for his very self in the gutters of mankind. Still, the three sisters have managed to win the last laugh despite his once mastery over their domain. Even so, the apple of long life lies secreted in the hearts of men. If they believe, time will not end, and with time, he will find the missing piece to solve the puzzle. Is he the last? The answer to that question remains unknown. Has the first cycle of ending finished yet or is it still to happen? He does not know. Has he been reborn or is he waiting to be devoured, swallowed whole? Even with an eye surrendered he is unable to tell. He needs time. He needs the best of mankind.

Odin the All-father. Father to both gods and man. Once master of the endless halls of Valhalla. Ruler of Asgard. Recognised through the ages by many names and associated with healing, death, wisdom, battle, poetry, and the runic symbols of power and sorcery. He is also believed to be the leader of souls. From his throne, Hlidskialf, in the tall tower where he dwells, his all-seeing eye surveys the nine worlds. He can see the fate of all humans and understand their past. He knows that a great ending is coming and pursues knowledge and wisdom relentlessly seeking a way to delay it. Due to this, he is known as the Wanderer and disappears from the sight of his peers for lengthy periods on quests only known to himself. His ever-present companions are the black ravens, Huginn 'thought' and his favourite, Muninn 'memory' who fly to his ears the latest news from all points of the world. Along with these are his faithful wolves, Geri 'the ravenous' and Freki 'greedy one' who eats the food from his hands as he has no need for such sustenance. In his hand, he carries a magical spear, Gungnir 'the swaying one', into whose sacred ash he has carved his secret runes.

'Oh, how are the mighty fallen and their weapons of war perished.'

Odin, most celebrated of the gods, now wanders lost and diminished in a world he helped create from the body of his murdered father.

If we take the time to have a hard look into places we do not wish to see, we may catch a glimpse of him as he struggles not to fade into the ether between the worlds.

THE END

ABOUT THE AUTHOR

The author has the bones of ten books arranged in his imagination. His aim is to write them all within three years. 'I ONCE WAS' is his fifth to come into realisation. He is already working on the next.

You can follow the author on
https://www.amazon.com/author/jcpereira

34722911R00078

Printed in Poland
by Amazon Fulfillment
Poland Sp. z o.o., Wrocław